He ran the tip of the spoon along Luci's lower lip.

Her tongue followed the motion to chase any specks of the fruity goodness that might have lingered. Then he abruptly took the spoon away, and the tip of her tongue darted out to try to catch it, though it was gone. Gio's soft laugh shot straight into the base of her belly.

"Are you ready?" He brought the spoon back to tease her lips apart again. Her eyes involuntarily popped open. His smiling face, together with the nod he gave her, was an unspoken direction to close them again. Which she did, with a slow breath in that filled her lungs with the fragrance of the shop.

At the next creamy offering, she rolled the gelato around her mouth again. "Chocolate. A dark chocolate at that."

"Taste more," he said as he fed her another bite.

"Delicious."

"Exquisite."

"Did you have some?"

"No. I was talking about..." He stopped himself.

Dear Reader,

Florence, Italy. Ah, the mere thought of that city makes me swoon. I've been lucky enough to visit twice and I cherish the memories. I was eager to set a romance there so that you and I could be transported to the City of Lilies (although I don't recall actually seeing any lilies there), where we'll meet Princess Luciana of fictional Izerote and billionaire Gio Grassi. Who both have a lot of reasons not to fall in love.

Blame it on Florence...

Handsome and brilliant Gio is returning to his childhood home after living all over the world. Lovely Luciana has come to Florence to do some living before the life changes that await her at the palace. In the city where so much intellectual and creative thought has occurred throughout history, these two grapple with the big questions of what it means to be free and how priorities order us, rather than the other way around. Loyalty versus discovery. Duty versus desire.

Along the way, we're exploring the land of Michelangelo's masterpieces, bustling piazzas and a certain gelato-eating session that I hope will leave you longing...for romance.

Andrea x

The Italian's Runaway Princess

Andrea Bolter

Recycling programs for this product may not exist in your area.

ISBN-13: 978-1-335-13530-8

The Italian's Runaway Princess

First North American publication 2018

This edition published by arrangement with Harlequin Books S.A.

For questions and comments about the quality of this book, please contact us at CustomerService@Harlequin.com.

Printed in U.S.A.

Andrea Bolter has always been fascinated by matters of the heart. In fact, she's the one her girlfriends turn to for advice with their love lives. A city mouse, she lives in Los Angeles with her husband and daughter. She loves travel, rock 'n' roll, sitting at cafés and watching romantic comedies she's already seen a hundred times. Say hi at andreabolter.com.

Books by Andrea Bolter

Harlequin Romance

Her New York Billionaire
Her Las Vegas Wedding

Visit the Author Profile page at Harlequin.com.

For Ellen

Praise for
Andrea Bolter

"This is Ms. Bolter's debut novel though it doesn't show.... The characters are well rounded and have a touch of reality that allows them to flow off of the page and into our imaginations."

—*Harlequin Junkie* on *Her New York Billionaire*

CHAPTER ONE

HER ROYAL HIGHNESS Princess Luciana de la Isla de Izerote finally inhaled the warm air of Florence, Italy. The secret journey from her home, an island near the coast of Spain, had been difficult. At last she was under the Tuscan sun, the yellow glow much different from the seascape she was used to. But the liberation she expected to feel as she took her first breath of freedom was hardly as she'd hoped.

As a matter of fact, Luciana was starting to feel afraid being alone. She was short of breath from walking too fast away from the encounter at the jewelry store, where she had been unsuccessful in converting a palace ruby into a typical tourist's spending money. Worse still, three teenage boys seemed to be following her. Swiveling her head enough to take a look at them behind her, she saw they were scruffy and wore shabby T-shirts and track pants. These unexpected companions made her entire escape plan seem not only reckless, but like it was about to become dangerous.

"*Bambolina*, let us see your necklace," one of the boys called out as they closed the distance between themselves and the princess. "We'll buy your jewel."

Luciana hastened her pace. She'd arrived in Florence to have an adventure before she lived the rest of her life in royal duty. The escapade didn't include being chased by thugs who might be trying to steal the jewelry she'd brought with her to sell as a way to finance her trip, given that she had no actual money of her own. The princess quickened to almost a run as her hand clutched the ruby pendant that hung from a heavy chain. Her sense of direction turned all around, she didn't even know where she was headed.

The boys behind her may or may not have seen that she had other pieces of jewelry in the purse that hung from a long leather strap on one of her shoulders, crossing her body and slapping against her at the opposite hip as she rushed away from them. She might have been able to run faster had she not also been toting a wheeled suitcase that contained her belongings for her three weeks as a Florentine tourist. After which time, she'd return to

Izerote. And to her obligations, including her arranged marriage to King Agustin de la Isla de Menocita, the widower thirty years her senior from a neighboring island.

Princess Luciana had thought about this getaway for a long time, plotting exactly how she'd make her way to Florence and how she'd finance the travels. What she hadn't counted on was how problematic it would be to sell jewelry. Having had no experience, she didn't know that the shops would require paperwork and authentication.

After she'd made it from the island to her first stop in Barcelona, she'd needed the first installment of cash for the train tickets to Florence and to buy some food. One jeweler had directed her to another of less repute, and he to another still, until she'd sold an amethyst cocktail ring for far less than its worth.

She knew little about city streets, having spent most of her life behind the palace walls of Izerote. Leaving only to attend official engagements and social functions accompanied by palace security, she was always safely sequestered in private cars, boats and planes. That was exactly why she'd come to Florence, the place she'd fallen in love with through art, books and movies. To experience being a simple tourist, to wander here and there without an itinerary or bodyguards, was to be a once-in-a-lifetime dream.

Having trouble selling the jewelry and now being followed just after she'd arrived was turning it into a nightmare.

"Bella." One of the boys hurried even closer to her, his use of the endearment for *beautiful* sounding like a snake's hiss that terrified her.

"Signorina. *Carina. Tesoro...*" Another bounced around to the other side of her, trying every name he could think of to get her to stop and address him directly.

With a yank on her suitcase, she began to run faster, heart racing. She thought about calling out for help to the first person she saw, but she didn't want to attract attention to herself. Her tiny island country was not well-known to most the world, but nonetheless, if questioned, she was a princess and it would appear odd that she was alone on the streets of central Florence. No one knew she was here, and she wanted to keep it that way.

Turning a corner, the boys chased after her and one pulled on the strap of her purse.

"Stop. Leave me alone," Luciana cried out and broke free.

A part of her fully expected her father King Mario's security team to have outwitted her already, to know exactly where she was and to direct unseen bodyguards to arrive at any moment to whisk her back to Izerote without letting her have the grand escapade she'd planned. With these boys harassing her, she almost wished they would.

Thinking quickly, she worked in front of her stomach to block the boys' view as she removed the rest of the jewels from her purse and held them tightly in her free hand. If they managed to steal her purse, at least they would find it empty.

"You give us that purse, right now," one of the boys jeered in a threatening tone.

"Get away from me," Luciana shouted. She looked to see if anyone else was behind her, her suitcase wobbling. As she turned back around, she tripped over something on the ground and crashed right into...

The broad shoulders and chest of a man. Specifically, her face slammed directly into the center of the man's muscular chest. As she approximated where her nose hit into him, she estimated just how tall a man he was. Six foot three, at least. Her head involuntarily turned a bit sideways so that her cheek could replace her nose as she pressed against him. Because that exact spot was solid, warm, smelled like clean laundry, and she quite liked it. Although she knew she needed to bend her neck back in order to see the face of the man she'd crushed into, something in her resisted the idea and she simply wanted to nuzzle her face into his rock-hard chest for the foreseeable future.

"Hello," a voice from somewhere inside the man's body crawled into her. "Do you need help?" His very deep timbre completely enveloped her in muscles and sounds. He could be yet another foe, but it didn't feel that way.

One thing she knew for sure was that it was not the chest of King Agustin de la Isla de Menocita, the man she was to marry in three weeks. Not only was King Agustin much smaller in stature than the man she pressed into, her fiancé spoke in a voice high and clipped. Nothing like the smooth-as-cappuccino voice of the man her cheek was touching.

"These boys are trying to steal my purse." Princess Luciana spoke into the good-smelling man's chest, knowing that he'd be able to hear her even though her mouth was far lower than his ear. She clutched her jewels so tightly that her fingernails cut into her palms.

His response was to do what every fiber in her being had actually hoped he would since she bumped into him. He placed both of his long arms around her and pulled her into a tight hold, encircling her in the most complete way. *"Mia amata—"* he used the words of a lover "—you're so late. I was running to the train station to find you."

Realizing that he was pretending to be with her as a way to shake off these would-be criminals, Luciana knew enough to play along. "I stopped at the jewelry store."

"Can I do something for you gentlemen?" The pretend lover turned his attention to the thugs. The boys seemed to be taking stock of the situation now that the good-smelling man had arrived on the scene. Without answering, they lingered awhile longer. "I repeat, can I do something for you?" the man with the gigantic strong arms around the princess shouted in a voice menacing enough to scare them.

Luciana craned her neck so that she could look up to see the man's face. As if the mere feel of his chest and tone of his voice wasn't enough, she now stared at one of the most handsome men she had ever seen.

Pale skin served to draw extra attention to the sparkling light blue eyes. He had high cheekbones, a full red mouth and a head full of beautiful golden curls, like a subject in a painting from the Renaissance, an era when Florence was abuzz with intellectual, scientific and creative discovery. A time in history that was one of the reasons Luciana had wanted to explore this important city.

"Oh, no, signore," said one of the boys behind her.

"We were taking a walk on this lovely day," another singsonged.

Only after they scattered away did the man with the lavish blond curls let go of Luciana. They looked directly into each other's eyes for the first time. She thought she might have been struck by a bolt of lightning, but the sunny skies rendered that unlikely.

The blue-eyed man then began to disentangle the long purse strap that had become twisted around Luciana's arm after the boys tried to pull it away from her. The strap was so mangled it became a puzzle to unravel it, and he gave his full attention to the task. Finally, he gingerly placed the strap back on her shoulder and the purse fell naturally across her opposite hip as intended.

The care this total stranger was extending to her was surprising. And also a first for Princess Luciana. Commoners were not permitted to touch her, except on occasions of handshakes during official processionals through the streets or when meeting military heroes, and under close supervision. But certainly nothing involving a gorgeous man with enormous hands putting his arms around her or arranging a purse onto her body.

Only then did Luciana remember what she held in her still tightly closed fist. "Oh, my gosh, I'd forgotten that I'd been holding my jewels all of this time. I thought surely those boys were going to tear my purse off me, so I grabbed the contents."

"Why are you carrying such valuables in a flimsy purse on a city street?"

"It's a long story."

The princess opened her purse and placed her jewels in a zipped pocket inside. As the man with the gigantic hands said, it was absurd that she'd let the few palace jewels, which she had chosen as sacrificial lambs to buy her this voyage of freedom, be tossed around in a thin pouch of leather not properly protected. That was only one of the possibly crazy decisions she had made.

There was no turning back now.

"Thank you." She bowed her head to the Renaissance painting of a man on the street. "You saved me from danger and harm."

"That's me. A regular Prince Charming."

Her Royal Highness Princess Luciana de la Isla de Izerote had never wished harder that words were true.

* * *

"May I show you to your destination?" asked the handsome savior after the thugs were long gone from view.

"All right," Luciana answered although she didn't know what her destination was. Which, as she was zooming to Italy through Spain and France on high-speed trains, felt like a marvelous relief. To be able to go wherever she wanted, whenever she wanted. Not to be bound by a schedule or accompanied by an entourage. Now, the unfamiliarity of all that liberty had her frightened.

"By the way, I'm Gio. Giovanni Grassi. And you are...?" He took hold of Luciana's suitcase handle and gave it a tug.

"Luci..." She left it at that, the nickname her mother used to call her when she was a small child. A name she hadn't heard in years. It was fitting that she thought of her mother now, who had died without ever fulfilling her own quest for the bit of autonomy that Luciana hoped to have.

"It's a pleasure to meet you, Luci."

She wasn't sure that she should be letting this man she didn't know pull her suitcase. What if he ran away with it? Or what if he was luring her into some kind of trap so that he could steal her jewels for himself?

Princess Luciana sensed that he meant well. After all, no one had forced him to come to her aid as he did. And she couldn't just continue standing on the street now that those threatening boys had been chased off. She'd lost all sense of direction, not that she knew where she was going in the first place. Had she been able to sell the ruby, she would have returned to the train station to look for a tourist bureau that could help her find accommodations. That could still be her plan. But now she wasn't comfortable walking alone with the jewels.

So they began forward, Gio's grip on her suitcase keeping its wheels cooperating under his control. Princess Luciana caught a reflection of herself in the glass of a shop window. In the commotion of her arrival, her failure at the jewelry store near the train station and the threat from those boys, she'd completely forgotten that she wore a wig in disguise. While Izerote was not a famous island and her monarchy had not made her a recognizable face throughout the world, she knew there was a good chance that her father would send someone looking for her. Even though she had left him a note promising to return in three weeks to marry King Agustin as planned. If the cloak she donned could help throw any operatives of King Mario's off her track, it was well worthwhile. Plus, she liked the idea of having a new appearance.

Gone were the long girlish locks of hair that spent many evenings as a showplace for the family tiaras. Now the thick brown strands that fell halfway down her back were bound and tucked under a blond wig she'd bought in Barcelona. The wig was cut into a lob, a term the princess knew from idly flipping through fashion magazines was the hip description for a long bob.

The surprisingly realistic-looking hairstyle fell in sleek sheets to the tops of her shoulders where it curled under just a bit. Every move she made caused the lob to give a slight swish that Luciana found chic. The hair made her feel like a woman on the go. Which was quite unlike the fussy preplanned existence she had always known. Although her *let's see what happens* attitude, so out of character, had almost led her into hazard.

"Where to, signorina?"

The scare of those boys had been an immediate awakening to the perils she needed to look out for, and she didn't know what she should tell Gio Grassi. Yes, his beautiful crystal-blue eyes seemed trustworthy, but outward appearances told her nothing.

Nonetheless, she had to start somewhere.

"I don't know, Gio. I find myself arriving in Florence with less money than I had planned. Would you know of a reasonably priced hotel?"

"No, actually, I'm sorry I don't. I grew up here in Florence but I've spent many years traveling for business. I no longer know the city."

Disappointment rung through her. Barcelona had been quite an eye-opener once she discovered that the jeweler to whom she had intended to sell the first of her lot was unwilling to buy what Luciana referred to as her *estate pieces* without proof of ownership and certifications. She'd made up a story about the jewels belonging to her recently deceased grandmother.

At her begging, that jeweler put her in touch with another jeweler who refused her and sent her to yet another, this one located in a downtrodden part of town. He gave her far less than she had estimated for the first piece. She knew now that this trip would have to be on more of a budget than she'd originally envisioned.

That didn't matter. At least she was here.

"I'll need to sell more of my jewels."

"More of them? Does that mean you have already sold some?"

Yes, but she didn't need to tell that to Gio.

"I had tried at a shop near the train station. That's where those boys began following me."

"Florence is a big city with people both opulent and poor, honest and not. You should watch out at every turn."

Luciana was already learning that the hard way. But as they turned a corner into a piazza, a public square, her troubles receded and the widest of smiles swept across her face. Here it was. The Florence she'd seen in movies and travel websites, and read about in books. Firenze, the central city of Tuscany, with its centuries of trade and finance, art and medicine, religion and politics.

People moved across the piazza in every different direction. Fashionable girls giggled as they snapped selfies of themselves. A tour group of older travelers dutifully stopped so that their guide could point out landmarks. Four men stood in front of a shop arguing, their loud voices and hand gestures marking them as uniquely Italian. A flock of children chased pigeons, their overjoyed faces bursting with surprise every time one of the birds made an unexpected escape. Two lovers sat close on a bench while they shared a fresh orange, the woman holding the peel in her hand.

Every which way, people wove in between each other to get to where they were going. It was everything the princess had imagined it would be, alive and magnificent under the autumn of the Tuscan sky. She placed her hand over her mouth as she took it all in.

This was what Luciana came to see. To be a part of this city that had always held her fascination, if only for a stolen moment of her lifetime. She drew in a slow breath. The air wasn't as thick and pure as it was in pristine Izerote. Florence had a particular fragrance, one she suspected it had for centuries.

It smelled like free will.

Which she had never inhaled before.

As if the panorama of all these people and their doings and their businesses and their architecture and their dogs wasn't enough, Luciana stood witnessing it in the company of a chivalrous, and she had to acknowledge gorgeous, Italian man.

For the first time she took notice of what Giovanni Grassi was wearing. A tweed blazer with a pink button-down shirt and tan tie, jeans with a brown belt and brown oxford shoes. All of impeccable quality. He looked perhaps like a young professor, the type schoolgirls would giggle around but loved to gape at as he explained the important trigonometry equation on a chalkboard behind him. Reluctant hottie. That was the moniker the celebrity websites used for his type.

Hottie, for sure. Reluctant, she didn't know yet.

"Ah yes, Firenze," Gio chimed in. "There's nowhere like it in the world. Some things change, others remain the same as they have for centuries."

Nothing ever changed in Izerote, Luciana reflected. It lagged far behind the rest of the world in technology and culture and commerce. Her father, King Mario, and his father before him were not forward-thinking rulers like some royal families were. The price they'd paid for the lack of progress was steep, as many residents or their adult children were leaving the island.

However, Princess Luciana was not in Florence to solve the issues of her island, although she didn't doubt that in this great city of thought and industry many dilemmas of the world had been debated.

"Here's my situation, Gio," Luciana started, not knowing what to do about her predicament. One way or another, this trip would come to an end. Either she'd have her three weeks here before she returned to Izerote to marry King Agustin and produce his heirs. Or her father would send someone to hunt after her and her visit would be cut short. Either way, now was all there was, so she had better make every second count. "I have no money. That's why I need to sell some of my jewels, in order to pay for a hotel room."

"Sell your jewels. That sounds so positively archaic. You may have noticed this is *modern day* where people pay for goods and services with credit cards or through apps on their phone," he said with a cute chuckle that sent a tingle down her spine. What a strange reaction she was having to this total stranger.

She couldn't explain to him that while she did carry credit cards, she couldn't use them because they were traceable. That's why she needed to obtain cash for the trip. "I know, it does sound rather medieval."

"Have you traveled forward in time? What era are you from?"

"You have no idea how right you are."

"Are you running from something?"

"You could say that."

"A mystery woman."

"You could say that, too."

"All right, Signorina Luci, if that's really

your name. For how long do you need a hotel room?"

"Three weeks," she answered with ease. Because it was exactly three weeks and one day until she was to marry. Three weeks. That's how long she hoped to stay in Florence. If she had her druthers, she'd stay until the last possible minute and arrive back in Izerote just in time to be pinned into her wedding gown. The gown that had already been chosen for her, a chaste lacy puffball with a high neck and long sleeves that was as tight and confining as her impending marriage. Nothing like what she'd wear if the choice was up to her. If, for example, she was to be getting married of her own volition to a tall attractive man with sparkling blue eyes and golden curly hair.

"Three weeks," he repeated. "And how much do you expect to garner from the sale of those jewels?"

Nowhere near what she thought she might, Luciana mused. So, realistically, considering the price she'd fetched in Barcelona, she quoted Gio a figure. Still unsure if she should be confiding her financial woes to him.

"Twenty-one nights…"

"Twenty-one," she confirmed knowing that she wouldn't need a hotel room in Florence on the twenty-second, after her wedding. She winced at the thought of her wedding night and what would be expected of her from King Agustin, a widower who presumably had more experience in the matrimonial bed than she did. Hopefully he'd be patient and compassionate toward her when the time came.

"Then here is how much you'd have to spend each day." Gio performed a mental calculation and gave her a number that was far less than the rate of the hotels she had been looking at online.

"Do you think I could get a hotel room for that price? It doesn't need to be fancy, only clean."

"Luci, for that money I don't think you could find anything suitable, clean or safe."

He glanced at his watch.

It wasn't right to detain this man any longer, despite the fear that was returning in her.

"I'll figure something out. Thank you again for your assistance."

"You're quite welcome. Enjoy Florence," Gio said and then turned to walk away.

Prompted by his departure, a couple of tears smarted Luciana's eyes as she blinked them back. Which was ridiculous. She'd come to experience Florence alone. Gio had simply lent a hand to a damsel in distress. He was a stranger, now on his merry way as was appropriate.

After a few steps, he stopped and pivoted back.

"What are you planning to do?"

"I don't know. If you could point me in the direction of the train station, I'll go back there."

"I can try to find you a hotel. Let's get off the street. Come with me."

"Oh. No. I'll be fine."

He furrowed his brow. "Very well, then. Goodbye, Luci."

"Goodbye."

But when he walked away again, anxiety gripped Luciana's chest. Those boys had really scared her. And not having the cash she needed was a huge problem. She hadn't pictured herself alone and lost on the street.

"Gio," she blurted out, quickly catching up with him. "Thank you. I would appreciate your help."

Gio stopped in front of a large building with double doors made of oak, each bearing a brass doorknob. Although the structure was hundreds of years old, the fob entry system was proof it had been updated. When the tiny red light on the mechanism turned to green,

Gio opened the door and held it wide for Luci to enter. Pulling her suitcase in with him, he then closed the door behind him. He led her through the stone tunnel passageway that kept the inner property well secluded from the busy streets of Florence.

The tunnel was a short distance, allowing Gio to see the sunshine that met it at the other end. He and his brother, Dante, used to play all sorts of games in this tunnel when they were kids.

"Where are we?" Luci asked with understandable trepidation.

"My home," Gio said as they came into the light of the central courtyard.

"Your home?" Luci began to take in the surroundings.

"My family's home. No one is here right now, but yes, this is where I grew up."

Up until a few days ago, Gio hadn't been home in many months. As the president of research, development and project management for his family's company, Grasstech, the world's largest manufacturer of computer components, Gio spent his life traveling among the company's operations centers all over the world. He touched down in Florence for crucial in-person meetings or for family occasions, but was then soon boarding a plane to his next destination.

"This is so beautiful," Luci exclaimed as she did a slow 360-degree turnaround in the inner courtyard of the villa compound.

"It's been in our family for six generations."

Indeed, Villa Grassi was a special place. It wasn't a showy high-tech complex befitting the Grassi family's standing in the computer science world. Instead the property retained its old-world charms, thanks to Gio's mother, although with plenty of modern conveniences. The villa comprised several stone buildings, all painted in a mustardy yellow color accented by the red terra-cotta roofs and wood trim.

"You live here?" Luci asked, still taking in the details of the central garden.

Mamma mia, but this young woman was pretty. Not just pretty, really, although Gio struggled for the right word to describe her. *Soulful*, maybe. There was depth in her light brown eyes. They were eyes with questions, eyes that longed. The dark, thick eyebrows that crowned those lovely pools served to set off their radiance even more. The sleek blond hair read as stylish, not that Gio knew much about fashion. Her petite frame was dressed with polish in her black skirt and gray blazer.

Why did this upscale-looking young woman have only jewels and no money? Something was quite off here, which Gio found suspicious. He would forever keep up his guard after the disastrous mistake he'd made in Hong Kong by trusting the wrong person. People weren't always who they said they were.

It seemed all but impossible that this woman in front of him could have somehow staged the incident with the boys on the street so that she could bump into him. That she had known where he was coming from and where he was headed. However, he'd learned the hard way that some people would say or do anything to get what they were after. Danger came in all shapes and sizes.

"I didn't understand what you said. Do you live here?"

"Not since childhood," he answered, still sizing her up. "But now I am home, so it seems."

The two-story main house anchored the buildings. Five steps led to the front door, constructed of the same oak as the door to the street. He looked up to the second-floor window that was his boyhood bedroom. Like all the windows, the sill was adorned with boxes holding plants in bright reds, oranges and yellows befitting the fall season. Beside it was the window in his brother Dante's bedroom.

Late at night they'd tie up sheets to hold on to and swing into each other's bedrooms like Tarzan. Gio smiled at the antics of his dare-devil brother, who hadn't changed a bit even as an adult.

In the courtyard, a cast-stone fountain gurgled with water, surrounded by the benches where his grandparents used to spend their afternoons. His grandfather would good-naturedly yell at Gio and Dante to slow down as they played their racing games in the tunnel. Their grandmother, content to sit for hours with her needlework, would ply the boys with blood orange juice from their fruit trees to drink, the color of which was still Gio's favorite hue in the world.

"We use the cottages now." Gio pointed to the two outbuildings beside the house, both of which had entrances that faced the courtyard.

"You said *we*. Who is we?"

"My brother, Dante, and I. And other relatives who come to stay. My parents still live in the big house when they're here, but we have a vineyard and winery in the country-side where they spend most of their time now that they've retired." His father had built Grasstech from a small purveyor of computer central processing units, known as CPU chips, into the multibillion-dollar conglomerate it was today. "Dante is working with our affiliates in India, now that…"

Gio was glad he stopped himself. Luci didn't need to know that Dante had failed at helming the company, which was why Gio had returned to Florence to do just that. Oversharing information had gotten him into trouble in the past, some of which he still needed to find a way to clean up.

In the silence of stopping himself, he focused on Luci's attentive face. There was something utterly enchanting about her, with that long stately neck and those curious eyes. She was much shorter than he had noticed at first. Of course, with him so tall, almost everyone was petite to him. Her bowed pink lips complemented her porcelain skin. Her posture was so straight and that throat so graceful she could pass for a noblewoman or a young duchess. Yet she had an inner spunk that made the thought of her as a stuffy royal thoroughly implausible.

Good heavens! Women should be the last thing on Gio's mind now that he'd returned home with a to-do list a mile long. And it was a woman who had got the company into trouble in the first place. He would be staying far away from them.

"That's the Duomo!" Luci pointed to the

top of the dome visible in the distance past the villa walls. Florence's cathedral was one of the most identifiable sights in the city.

"Have you been inside?"

Her enthusiasm was contagious.

"No. I'm looking forward to seeing it. This is my first time in Florence. You rescued me just as I arrived."

A little wiggle traveled between his shoulder blades when she said the word *rescued*.

Now that he had, in fact, rescued her, what was he going to do with her? He'd find her a hotel. But some of Grasstech's investors were in town for dinner and he needed to get dressed, so it had to be quick. He wasn't looking forward to all their chitchat that bored him to tears. Nothing of substance was ever discussed at these things. Plus they'd all be bringing their stodgy spouses. The wives would ask why a nice young man like him didn't have a wife or a girlfriend.

With enough on his mind already, Luci's problems couldn't become his. Yet she'd been so shaken by those nasty boys following her, she finally accepted his offer of help.

She readjusted her purse on her shoulder, the one that contained her jewels. "May I ask you, Gio, would there be *any* hotel at *any* price that you could recommend for the night? I'll have to reevaluate my budget, but I do need somewhere for tonight."

He could give it a try. Pulling his phone out of his jacket pocket, he punched in a hotel search, hoping he'd recognize the names of some that were reputable.

"Yes," he spoke after calling one. "Do you have any rooms available for tonight? I see. *Grazie.*"

He phoned another. "Have you a room tonight? No? *Grazie.*" After three more, his patience was up.

"That's all right, Gio," Luci said, although the quaver in her voice belied her words. "I'll find somewhere."

With her obvious lack of street savvy? What if some other criminals tried to take advantage of her like the boys did with the jewelry? He might not know this vulnerable young woman, but a gentleman was a gentleman and he could not send her away alone.

"Why don't you stay here tonight?" Gio voiced the thought that had been bubbling up, despite raising caution. "I'm staying in this one." He pointed to one of the side-by-side cottages. "Why don't you sleep in the other?" He hoped that suggestion wouldn't prove to be a mistake, but he couldn't think of what else to do. He'd station her here, and the staff at his office could help get her situated tomorrow.

"Oh, no, I couldn't." Luci quickly shook her head with a side-to-side motion. "It wouldn't be right."

He put his hand over his heart in mock insult. "What do you take me for? I assure you I offer only to fulfill my quota of rescuing beautiful maidens from the mean streets of Florence."

Was he *flirting* with her?

"How are you doing so far?"

"I'm desperately behind. You'd be helping me out."

She looked at him with a bite to her lip. He knew she was deciding on his merits versus his potential risks.

"I'll only consent if you let me repay you in some way."

The idea quickly fell from his lips. "I have a very dull dinner with some investors to attend tonight. They will have no doubt chosen the poshest restaurant in Florence with a continental menu that manages to avoid anything authentically Italian. They'll pick an impressive bottle of wine chosen for its price and torture the sommelier as they swirl it around in their glasses pretending to know something about the vintage. They'll discuss the weather and the latest political scandal in Italy, and it will make watching paint dry sound compelling. Would you like to join me?"

"With an invitation like that, how could I possibly refuse?" Luci answered with a huge smile that shot straight into Gio's heart. He returned the grin.

Once he'd extended the invitation to dinner, it suddenly sounded like a marvelous idea. She was far more interesting than the blah-blah-blah he'd have to exchange with the investors. Rightly, they'd save any substantial conversation for boardroom conferences.

Why shouldn't he have a pleasant evening with an attractive woman? He knew he'd never take it any further than that. It was just dinner. And bringing her with him was better than leaving her alone on his property tonight. He'd get her out of the villa in the morning.

"It's set then? Pick you up right here?" He gestured to the fountain.

"I have a cocktail-length dress. Will that be sufficient?"

"And obviously you can accessorize." He pointed to the purse with all of the jewels. "You'll be the toast of the town."

"I hope not." Luci's eyes opened in alarm.

"I was only joking. See you at eight."

CHAPTER TWO

"THANK YOU, VIGGO." Gio acknowledged his driver as he parked the car in front of the villa. Viggo quickly got out of his seat and dashed around to the passenger side to open the door for Luciana and Gio. After Gio helped her out of the car, she straightened the skirt of the pale blue dress she'd worn to dinner with him and his investors.

It was her little secret that she'd chosen the dress to complement the color of her handsome companion's eyes. Of course, the color of Her Royal Highness Princess Luciana's dress for the evening was the least of her secrets. Nonetheless, with her cool blond wig, silver shoes and diamond earrings, she felt like a woman who had been on a real date with a real man, as opposed to a shielded virgin locked in a stone tower. Gio had quickly become part of her grand adventure.

"Do we have to go in?" Luciana touched

Gio's jacket sleeve as he reached in his pocket for his fob entry to the wooden exterior door.

"Would you like to walk?"

"I'd love to."

Driving from the restaurant after the dinner, Luciana was agog as they drove past landmarks she wanted to visit while she was here. The incredible piazzas, historic churches, marketplaces, museums and neighborhoods she'd seen only as an armchair traveler in the solitude of her palace sitting room. While she'd traveled to many places in the world for ceremonies and royal engagements, she'd never seen them as a tourist, able to meander and linger, and appreciate anything that caught her fancy. She could hardly wait to get started.

"Let's walk this way." Gio gently placed his hand on the small of her back to direct her away from the villa door. Her awareness arched to meet his touch.

"Thank you for accompanying me to dinner. As I mentioned, I generally leave the finessing of investors to my brother, Dante, now that our father has retired."

"And Dante was unable to attend tonight?"

"Dante is spending some time at our offices in Mumbai. We have restructured the company and I will now serve as CEO."

"What did you do before?"

"Product development. Which is where my heart is. You'd find me happier trying to make an AGP bus that can carry graphics faster than anything else on the market than you would seeing me in a conference room."

"AGP?"

"Accelerated graphics port."

"Of course," she joked. "How would I not know that?"

"But now I'll do what needs to be done for the company. Actually, I welcome the opportunity to do things my way. To get them right."

"Are things not right?"

"Look at those two." Gio pointed to two dogs on leashes across the street that barked at and sniffed each other with great interest.

Ah, Luci noted, she had asked too snoopy a question about Gio's work and he'd changed the subject. Her inner Princess Luciana should have known better than to pry, in spite of her curiosity to know more about him.

She hoped to recover with, "Your investors were a lovely group of people. I saw photos on many a smartphone of grandchildren performing in school plays and rosebushes that had yielded prizewinners."

The princess was only too used to smiling

and taking interest in the lives of total strangers. In fairness, she was always quite honored that people she met wanted to share details about their lives with her. Meeting people was one of the things she did like about royal life. But not as much as she liked this, walking in the open air with Gio, and not a handler or schedule in sight.

"Enough about me," he said as they continued after watching the dogs perform mating rituals. "What do you do for a living?"

"I'm a teacher," Luciana fibbed. That was what she would be if she could. Royal duties combined with her father's outdated ways kept her ambition from coming to fruition. "I spend most of my days talking to four-year-olds."

"A teacher? I never would have figured you for that."

"Why not?"

"You're very—" he searched for the right word "—elegant. The way you handled yourself at dinner was distinguished. Well, there we go when we stereotype or pigeonhole anyone. My apologies."

If he only knew. How badly she didn't want to always have to be elegant. How her father raised her in a very old-fashioned monarchy she didn't question, where Luciana had been groomed her whole life to make appearances. To never share anything of herself, her hopes, her likes. To be only in the service of the crown. While she led a life of luxury and privilege for which she was grateful, her heart ached for more.

Perhaps she'd be content if the man she was to marry wasn't so much older and who, in the handful of meetings she'd had with him, hadn't talked to her as if she were already his possession. Maybe her life would be sublime if she was to wed a bold and good-humored man like say, just for example, Gio.

She blushed at her own thought as she noted the shadows the night sky cast onto Gio's defined cheekbones.

"*Bellissima*, what is a teacher doing traveling alone with only a bag full of jewels to pay her way?"

As she had learned in her years of training, restraint was always the best policy, so rather than answer him, she occupied herself taking in the light of the moon and how it played against not only Gio's face but also the architecture of this great ancient city.

"Where are you from, Luci?" Gio pressed.

"Spain," she simplified.

She had a flush of concern that she was out late at night in a foreign country with a man she'd only just met. Half of her considered the potential danger, but the other half wanted to throw caution to the wind and grab as many experiences as she could out of this trip to Florence. Including this unexpected interlude with a beguiling man.

"Your Italian is flawless."

"I studied for many years."

Indeed, Princess Luciana had always been fascinated with Italian history, art and literature, especially the Renaissance period when Florence was the center of Europe. It was a thrill to finally use the language she had practiced so diligently. While she had been to Rome for royal occasions and adored it, the City of Lilies had always held her interest.

About a year ago, her father, King Mario, had informed her that she would be marrying widower King Agustin of the neighboring island Menocita. She didn't protest, always wanting to please her father after her mother had died.

Izerote was racked with problems. Because theirs was a tiny country with limited development, unemployment had become a crisis. As the current generation had grown, many households sent their offspring away for higher education or to seek jobs in Spain or the rest of the world. Without careers on the island for future generations, the population would continue to shrink.

On Menocita, King Agustin's father had brought tourism to their shores. Exclusive resorts along with family-friendly water sports and vacation rentals had turned the island into a year-round paradise that created thousands of jobs for the inhabitants. After King Agustin's wife died, he'd decided to find another island to merge with to create the same tourism and bring larger prosperity to his family name. When the proposal of marriage to his daughter came to King Mario, he could not refuse. In turn, Princess Luciana could not let her father or her subjects down, so she had no option but to agree to it.

Yes, a future she wouldn't have chosen for herself was looming. But at least she'd always have this. Florence. This journey of self-discovery and of making a single dream come true.

Luciana did feel badly that she had left her father a note saying only that she would return to Izerote to marry King Agustin, but that she was going to do this one thing before she did. She had previously begged him to let her, just once, leave the island without attendants, limousines and security details. It was a liberty she needed to know, if even for a short time. It was something she longed for, a wanderlust she wasn't able to silence. King Mario, an overly protective man especially after her mother was killed in a car accident in Madrid, denied her. And not wanting to cause him anymore grief, she acquiesced—until she could no longer.

She thought back to the trip to Paris King Mario did plan for Luciana and a cousin her age. When they were there, clothing stores were closed to the public so that they could shop alone, never paying for anything. When the girls walked down the boulevards, bodyguards trailed only a few paces behind. An entire hotel floor was rented despite their needing only two rooms. They visited a museum after midnight, fully staffed for just the two of them. While Luciana did appreciate her father's efforts, it was hardly what she'd had in mind.

With the wedding imminent, Princess Luciana's heart, her soul, the very essence of her being, insisted that she break away from the protocol that had been drilled into her. And drove her to do something completely for herself, as reckless as it was. So, she escaped the palace walls and her role as the perfect daughter and princess, leaving no hint of where she was going. She bought no tickets for her transportation, brought along no phone where her location could be traced. As drastic a step as it was to take palace jewels to sell, she hadn't been able to think of another way.

Three weeks that belonged only to her wasn't so very much to ask for.

After her walk with Gio and their return to his villa, Luciana was tired. She'd face the issues of the jewels and finding a suitable place to stay tomorrow. For tonight, she was eternally grateful for his generosity.

They lingered at the halfway point between her guest cottage and his.

"I can't thank you enough for this."

"My pleasure, Luci. Thank you for accompanying me to the dinner." He crossed an arm over his waist and bowed forward to her in an exaggerated posture of formality that might have been funny if she was a different person.

"Did you sleep well?" Gio called up to Luci as she stepped out onto the small Juliet balcony of the guest cottage, wrapping her hands around the wrought iron railing. Properly known as a *balconet*, it wasn't large enough for a chair or table. It was meant for enjoying the view of the courtyard below and to peer out beyond the villa's walls. When Shakespeare included the architectural feature in his romantic tragedy, the nickname stuck.

It took considerable effort for Gio to pretend not to notice how the transparent fabric of the flowing white nightgown Luci wore hid nothing of her lovely curves underneath. But the sudden twitch in his core told the truth.

He placed the pot of coffee he was holding onto the small glass table near the fountain. "Would you like to join me for breakfast?"

"How magical to wake up and smell all of these flowers," Luci said with a sweeping arm surveying the courtyard's garden. "The lavender is so sweet."

The same view was available from Gio's bedroom, as the two cottages were identical. He had risen early and let himself into the main house to find some breakfast.

He glanced up to Luci again. It was actually nothing short of surreal that a beautiful woman stood on the balcony of his guesthouse in Florence, albeit that her status there was temporary. Surreal even that he was back home, as most of his adult life thus far had been spent living away. The idea of staying in one place might take some getting used to. "Come down and have some coffee."

Luci accepted the bid with, "Just give me a few minutes to get dressed."

An unfamiliar voice inside Gio wanted to beg her to come down as she was, so fetching did she look in her cotton gauze. But decorum won out.

Always buried in work, he had not been alone with a woman in quite a while. In spite of the fact that this unexpected maiden with the blond hair and the big brown eyes had landed in his lap yesterday, this was a very important morning. Which was why he'd chosen to wake at dawn, go for a run, shower and dress, all the while leaving himself enough time to have a relaxed breakfast.

Today was his first official day as CEO of Grasstech.

He stepped into his cottage to gather a laptop and some briefings he had been looking over and brought them out to the courtyard so he was ready to leave after breakfast. The two cottages were small but sufficient with a sitting room on the first floor, and a bedroom and bathroom upstairs. They were decorated in yellow, black and gold with expensive, but simple, furnishings. Gio's mother had told him that she'd recently redone the guest quarters and looked forward to his seeing them. Later, he'd ring her at the vineyard to offer his compliments.

Such coziness was unfamiliar to him. President of research, development and project management, Gio Grassi was accustomed to traversing the world, and preferred the anonymity of hotels. Sleek, modern hotel rooms looked no different to him whether he was in Cape Town or Seoul or Dallas. Hotels perfectly suited the life he had been leading. Everything at his disposal and on his own time clock.

When he was lost in concentration on a new project it could be hours, sometimes even days, that would pass while he was surrounded by computer parts and algorithms. He lived immersed in a technological world most people had no understanding of. Where he laid his head to rest was of little concern to him. Until now, when his entire lifestyle was about to change.

Gio hopped up the five steps from the courtyard to the main house to fetch the rolls and fruit the housekeeper had left for him. When he brought them to the outdoor table, Luci was coming out her front door, suitcase and purse in tow. In the morning sun, her eyes caught glints of light.

"Is something wrong?" she asked in reaction to his expression.

"Please, sit." He pulled out a chair for her to take her place at the table.

After coffee was poured and rolls were bitten into, Luci asked, "You're going to the Grasstech office today?"

"Yes. I've got to go be the boss man now," Gio said with a titter belying his mixed feelings on the transition. On one hand he was relieved to be taking full control of Grasstech and knew he would fine-tune operations and move the company even further forward. Yet the other side of him rather dreaded becoming the face of the empire. He'd made a mistake that had cost the company dearly and he had a lot of mopping up to do. In trusting his ex-girlfriend, Francesca, there were now leaked company secrets to contend with and a press ready to bring that information public.

"Thank you so much for your hospitality. I'll leave right after breakfast, so don't let me add to your troubles."

"Have we settled where you are going?" he asked with a quick glance at his watch. As strangely intriguing as this domestic scene was, he had a million other things on his mind. He wouldn't be finding out who this lovely Luci in front of him truly was. Not only didn't he have time for a woman in his life, he couldn't buy the story that she was a teacher. There was more going on with her than met the eye, and that was something he hadn't any business getting involved in.

"That's kind of you to consider my lodging something *we* are concerned about, but I'll figure it out on my own."

"Of course." But he couldn't leave it at that. Her mysterious identity notwithstanding, Gio's mother had taught him to be chivalrous, and after hearing yesterday about Luci's budget issues he wasn't going to have her traipsing alone around Florence looking for a cheap hotel that might not be safe.

"I'll have someone at my office look into hotels for you." The sooner he squared her safely away, the less he'd fret about it later.

"I couldn't impose like that."

"It's no imposition."

"Thank you but…it wouldn't be…"

If he let her go, he'd be distracted all day worrying if she was okay. And he needed his concentration today. "Why don't you go out and see some sights? We'll meet later and I can complain to you about my workday."

A giggle escaped from her, which brought a lovable little blush to her cheeks.

She had been an utterly flawless dinner date last night, charming his investors by laughing at their unfunny jokes and asking questions about their families to get them talking about themselves. Gio despised making small talk. Luci, who had appeared poised and almost regal in her blue silk dress, knew exactly how to field the evening, which took the pressure off him. He could return the favor. After that, she'd be out of his life and on with her holiday.

"It's settled, then. Why don't you leave your luggage here?" Gio stood and gathered up his things, having been alerted on his phone that his driver was here. "Where can my driver drop you?"

"I'll just wander out on my own."

He escorted her to the street. "See you here at six."

Gio's driver, Viggo, delivered him to the street-level glass doors of the Grasstech headquarters. The family kept a much larger campus of offices outside the city, but this central Florence location was where the company's important decisions were still made. Gio passed through to the main reception area where a few employees were congregating.

"Hello, Mr. Grassi," one greeted.

"Good morning, sir," another followed.

"Welcome, Mr. Grassi."

While he generally interacted with everyone he met on a first-name basis, he quite approved of the employees here addressing him formally at first. It was important to establish sole authority immediately.

That had been part of the problem with

his brother in the top seat. While he admired Dante as being more of a people person than he was—his brother had become a sort of brand ambassador for their company—Gio doubted he elicited much respect among the staff. Because, unfortunately, Dante spent more time being photographed with a different woman on his arm each evening at social functions than he did overseeing the company's operations. Whereas Gio understood the ins and outs of Grasstech's stronghold in the tech world and had specific plans on how to increase their dominance against the competition.

While Dante had been happy to use the press to his advantage, the media were actually Gio's first challenge of the day.

As he made his way down the corridor to the corner office that was originally his father's, Gio was aware of a pretty assistant in step beside him. Although she was an attractive young woman, Gio found his mind immediately flashed back to Luci's gracious smile as she engaged the older ladies last night with a discussion of favorite holiday memories. Something about Luci had gotten under his skin. Which he needed to put a stop to right away. The last thing he wanted to be embroiled with was a woman, especially now that deceitful Francesca was the cause of his most pressing problem.

"What can I get you, Mr. Grassi?" the assistant asked as she escorted him into his office.

"A large bottle of cold water. And send in Samuele, thank you."

"Yes, sir."

"Mio amico." Samuele di Nofri greeted Gio with a bear hug and affirmation of their lifelong friendship. The older man was Grasstech's director of operations and had been working with the company since the day Gio's father conceived of it. "Finally, we have you back in Firenze."

"Sit." Gio gestured to one of the leather chairs that faced his sleek steel desk.

"It was like yesterday that you were a boy, sitting at one of those desktop computers we used to keep here." Samuele pointed to a wall where a row of clunky old computers used to be lined up. Before everyone had laptops that weighed less than a cup of coffee. "Six years old and you would sit for hours writing code."

"Technology has come a long way since then."

"Grazie al cielo." Samuele kissed two fingers and lifted them to the sky.

"Although then, we didn't worry as much

about security and hacking. Now look what I caused the company to have to deal with."

"It happens."

Yes, Gio's early proclivity for computers had led him to eventually receive multiple degrees from Stanford University in California's Silicon Valley. Then after years of apprenticeship in Tokyo, he emerged as one of the world's most respected component designers.

What Gio's education and experience hadn't taught him was how to look out for Francesca and her kind. With her eight-foot-long legs and her crimson red lips, she was a skilled and practiced seductress. She had set her sights on the workaholic techie Grassi brother and had not relented until she'd got what she wanted. Which was not his heart.

No, what Francesca wanted were secrets about Grasstech's new memory modules that were destined to take drop-in compatibility wider than the industry had seen before. So while Gio was conceiving, designing, testing and troubleshooting, Francesca had done what she did best.

Francesca Nefando, who had been hired to run analytic reports, was actually a world-class hacker. In a tight skirt and high heels.

"Fine, Samuele, you say it happens." Gio grimaced at the memory of the day he found out his proprietary DIMMs, dual inline memory modules, were being developed by a rival company with information only an insider could know. Samuele's kindly eyes tried to offer some comfort. "But now that the industry press has found out, Grasstech could look weak in the field."

"That's why the board of directors tell me that they want you to issue a statement to the media. Because you are taking over as the CEO, they see this as an opportunity to solidify your name as the trailblazer of the company. That alone will help deflect the breach."

"Me? We have public relations people for this."

"Yes. But put it in your own words, Gio. It will sound authentic and announce your personal style of leadership."

He watched Samuele's mouth form words, but Gio was having a hard time actually listening. Because his blood was boiling thinking back to the strategy Francesca had designed to seduce him. Once he'd begun to trust her, she'd started to ask questions that required long nights of huddling together over a laptop in bed, her auburn hair almost sickly sweet from the gardenia-scented shampoo she used.

Francesca had taught him a lesson he

would never forget. He would never let anyone get that close to him again. But, weirdly, his thoughts meandered back to Luci this morning, so seemingly harmless as she stood on the balcony in her nightgown.

"What should I say in the press release? That I let a woman get the best of me?"

"No, Gio. Mull it over. You'll come up with something."

"Samuele, before you go. Can you look for a room at a decent hotel for about three weeks?"

Samuele regarded him quizzically.

"One of our investors isn't happy with where he's staying."

Gio took a deep breath. He had a full schedule and a multibillion-dollar company to run. So why was he already looking forward to seeing Luci again tonight?

"Drop us here," Gio instructed Viggo as the car approached the Piazza della Signoria. It had been ages since the piazza had been his destination. If he'd seen it at all during the past few years, it had been because he was merely crossing through to get to a meeting at an office or restaurant. Viggo let him and Luci out of the back seat.

Gio had decided to take her out. They'd

have dinner in one of the *osterias* whose piazza-facing patios would still be warm enough in the autumn evening.

"Oh, my gosh." Luci brought her hand over her mouth in genuine reverence as she took in the piazza. He could appreciate her sentiment, as it was one of Florence's most dramatic sights. In fact, historically, it had been the meeting place for all of Tuscany.

"There's the Fontana di Neptuno!" The marble-and-bronze Fountain of Neptune. "I've seen it in pictures so many times, I can't believe I'm finally here."

Luci's enthusiasm lightened Gio's mood after a long hard day of putting out administrative fire after fire in the remains of mistakes that Dante had made while he was at the helm. Mostly, though, he was still strategizing about the Francesca fiasco and its aftermath.

Still, he reiterated to himself that one of his goals when returning to Florence was to slow his pace a little and to enjoy relaxing pursuits. He worked too much; even his father thought so. A night out on the town with pretty Luci was just what the doctor ordered. Even though he had sworn never to get close to a woman again, it was only one evening. Okay, there was last night, too, but it was not as if he was going to devote his life to her.

Although when he presented a bent elbow for her to slip her arm through, he felt an unfamiliar lump at the bottom of his throat when she did so.

"Here is one of the fake *Davids*." She pointed to the replica of Michelangelo's masterpiece. "The original used to stand in this place but was moved to the Galleria dell'Accademia to protect it."

"You'll want to visit there."

"There's another replica of *David* in the Piazzale Michelangelo. The views of the city are supposed to be astounding from there."

"They are."

"And this is the Loggia dei Lanzi." The outdoor gallery of sculptures in the piazza.

"You've certainly studied up on the city. That way is the Uffizi Gallery—" he pointed a finger "—which, of course, you'll want to explore." One of the world's finest museums.

"Oh, yes." Her squeeze on his arm sent pricks of energy through his muscles.

"I can find a professional guide for you if you'd like."

"No. Thanks. I spend too much time already with guides and companions as it is."

"I take it you mean the children you teach? That's a cute way of describing them."

"Right." Luci's voice rose. "It does seem like

they are the ones leading the way most of the time."

At the restaurant he'd chosen, Gio asked the hostess to seat them outside facing the piazza. It was about as fine a night as could be with the dusk and the statues, Luci's face aglow with the breadth of it all.

"We'll have the prosciutto with melon, the mushroom risotto and the grilled *branzino*," he instructed the waiter. Gio was hungry so he ordered for them without consulting the menu. "Is that all right?" He turned to Luci.

"Yes. Thank you for asking."

"And we'll have a bottle of the Pallovana Frascati," Gio finished the order.

After the waiter returned with the Frascati, Luci asked, "You haven't told me anything about your first day yet. How did everything go?"

As they sipped their wine and took advantage of the superlative people-watching their vantage point on the piazza offered, he filled her in on reacquainting himself with staff and about some restructuring he was intending.

"My biggest problem is how to handle the information about a hack we experienced recently when the design for a product was obtained and sold to a competitor." The information about the hack was to soon be public knowledge, so he wasn't disclosing any secrets by talking to Luci about it.

"Has it been in the news?"

"Not officially. I know there's talk in the industry."

"Will you speak to the press about it?" That was exactly what Samuele had been urging this morning.

"I suppose I ought to before trade gossips do."

"So, should you issue a press statement?"

The waiter delivered plates with paper-thin slices of pink prosciutto draped across wedges of ripe orange melon.

"Grazie." Gio acknowledged the arrival and returned his attention to Luci.

"It was my own personal security that was weak in order for the hack to have happened. I gave clearance to someone I shouldn't have." Gio didn't want to tell Luci about Francesca specifically, so he kept it general.

"You don't want the company to appear compromised in the press," Luci said with her fork dangling in the air.

"Exactly. I'd like to think it was a grave mistake on my part but that, in general, our safeguards are very good. Nothing like that had ever happened before and hopefully never will again."

"Do you have any new products that are about to launch?"

"Why do you ask?" The question came out sharply. But here it was. This young lady who called herself a teacher from Spain could be, right under his nose, trying to get proprietary information from him under the guise of dinner conversation. That was how these charmers worked, wasn't it?

"I'm sorry, did I offend you?"

"Are you interested in computer science?" he baited, paying attention to every word.

"Not especially." She took a sip of her wine. "I was going to make a suggestion about your press release. Pardon me if I was being intrusive."

"Go on." He rubbed his chin as he continued to study her.

"What if you wrote a statement that wasn't strictly about the hack but was a *state of the company* address now that you've taken over? Then you can mention the leak and what security measures you're putting in place. But sandwich it in between news about the company's latest accomplishments."

"That's a great suggestion," Gio exclaimed. He thought immediately of the achievements he would like to announce, and that in the context of a report on the company they wouldn't come across as showboating. Indeed, his new peripheral component interconnect, PCI, was revolutionary.

Gio toasted Luci. As they clinked their wineglasses together it was as if they touched each other, a powerful sensation that traveled from his fingertips all the way up his arm to his heart.

They made it through the next two courses of their meal talking a mile a minute. Luci asked so many interesting questions about computers and listened patiently to techie mumbo jumbo that she surely didn't understand. Gio didn't reveal anything about his designs, and by the time dinner was over, his spy theory had lost steam. Luci was wonderful company.

The conversation continued as they stood in the courtyard of the villa under the night sky. "The random access memory, or RAM, is temporary," he finished the explanation he was giving her in the car.

"Your work is interesting."

The scent of the flowers in bloom permeated the garden.

Silence fell upon them.

The air between them stilled.

Her mood changed.

She'd spent dinner asking him about work

and had avoided talking about herself. He looked into her eyes to coax her on but she said nothing. She definitely harbored a secret, although he was now convinced it had nothing to do with him.

"Something is wrong?"

"Thank you again for your generosity."

It was as if the entire city was quietly holding its breath.

"You didn't tell me about your day. What sights did you see?"

With her head slightly bowed, she peered up at him through her eyelashes. "I'm embarrassed to tell you that I got completely lost. I was planning to visit the Piazza della Repubblica, but I ended up just sort of circling in a big loop. It was all beautiful, but I didn't see anything I had intended to."

Florence wasn't the easiest city to maneuver if you didn't know it, with streets jutting out from its many piazzas. Still, in this day and age, with all of the online resources and apps, a person should be able to find their way.

"You didn't use maps or tourist sites on your phone?"

She waited a beat before admitting, "I don't have a phone. I didn't bring one on the trip."

"*Bellissima*, is that even safe?"

"I wanted to unplug," she quickly responded,

"to truly be a wanderer without any trappings of real life. Besides…"

"Yes?" he prompted. Unplugging wasn't something he'd ever experienced, as his life revolved around being so very plugged in. Although it was something he needed to learn to do a little of.

"I'm not sure I should have come to Florence at all."

Gio stood firm and pierced his eyes into hers. "I can tell that you've come to Florence to lose yourself. That you're hiding something. Or hiding from something."

Luci scrunched her forehead. As if she was making a decision.

Then she reached to her head to run her fingers through her blond hair. Her hand moved farther and farther back until, with a tug, she lifted the blond hair completely off her head.

It was a wig! And from under the wig an avalanche of long brown waves cascaded down far past her shoulders.

"First of all, my name is not Luci. It's Luciana. I am Her Royal Highness Princess Luciana de la Isla de Izerote."

CHAPTER THREE

"*Brava.*" Gio used two fingers to mime tipping an imaginary hat toward Luci, or rather Princess Luciana. "That's quite a coup, a princess in disguise."

"You wouldn't believe it."

"Try me," he clipped. Luciana knew he would be upset to learn that she had pretended to be someone she wasn't, the deception made so much worse by the burn of the company hack he'd spoken of. He was quite sensitive during dinner when she'd asked about his upcoming products, as if he was suspicious of her and had been all along.

Now his jaw pulsed as he stood drilling into her with his big blue eyes, demanding an explanation.

"You've been so kind to me, Gio," she began constructing an apology. "I didn't expect to have a problem with selling my jewels. Then those boys were harassing me on the street and you came to my aid. And now you've given me this beautiful evening."

"You have an interesting way of showing your appreciation," he continued in a voice so low and tight she wasn't sure how the sounds were even escaping his throat.

Luciana fingered through the wig she held in her hand. The strands felt so fake despite how much she had liked wearing it. How silly it all seemed now, that she had tried to convince Gio she was a schoolteacher on a holiday. She supposed she had been trying that out on herself, a description of a woman and a life she could only imagine about.

"I'm so sorry. When I was sharing what I've learned about handling the media, you knew a schoolteacher wouldn't have any experience with that. I wanted to tell you the truth right then. I just didn't know how. I was trying to keep my identity hidden so that I could have just one anonymous adventure. I've never been on my own."

"I see."

"It's like what you're going through right now, having to transition from being a private to a public person. I've been in the palace my entire life. Although Izerote is not known to the rest of the world, on my own island I am under constant scrutiny."

Gio's expression slowly remolded from accusatory to something else, like he was truly listening to her.

"I'll just pack up my things and be out of your way." She turned from him to return to the cottage he'd been generous enough to let her stay in. She'd gather up as quickly as she could.

Over her shoulder she added, "Even though I have no right to, may I ask you one more favor? Could you not tell anyone about this? I would be eternally grateful if you forgot you ever met me."

As she swerved away, his big hand grabbed her arm.

"I didn't say you had to leave." Gio's voice kept its deep baritone but he didn't sound as angry anymore. "Please, Princess Luciana de la Isla de Izerote. Let me make us a cup of tea. I have to admit I'm intrigued. I've never hosted a real-life princess before. Let alone a runaway."

"I'm not made of fairy dust. Despite popular folklore."

If this had been a fairy tale, Gio Grassi could be her handsome prince. His armor would glisten as he swept her off her feet and hoisted her onto his proud white horse. Where they'd gallop away into the sunset to their kingdoms where marriages were conjured from love, not strategy.

"I'm dreading my entry into public life," Gio said. "So I do understand your desire for anonymity."

"That means a lot to me."

"You look quite different with your long and natural hair."

Luciana supposed she did. With her hair the same as she'd worn it her entire life she felt younger, like she was still a schoolgirl. How her father saw her.

"I actually love the wig," she confessed. "It's fashionable instead of how I usually look, stuck in time, born and bred to wear a tiara. What do you think?"

"Obviously, you should wear your hair however you want to."

His words stunned her. When was the last time anyone told her she should look however she wanted? Never.

"Shall we have tea?"

"Okay."

"I'll be right back."

As Gio went up to the main house, Luciana sighed with enormous relief. She couldn't have kept her identity a secret from him for a second longer. At first she thought he was so angry he was going to throw her out on the spot. Thank goodness his reaction changed. What a persuasive man he was. Her eyelids fluttered when he said she should do whatever she wanted with her hair.

Why couldn't she be marrying a compelling and progressive man like him? Why must she wed someone with a closed mind who had already told her that becoming pregnant was the first and only job he expected her to devote herself to? She did want children, but in all honesty, she dreaded the thought of giving her virginity to a man she would never love. That seemed a service past what was a reasonable expectation of any person.

"All right, Princess," Gio announced when he brought out two cups of tea and invited her to sit at the glass table in the courtyard where they'd had breakfast early that morning. "I want to hear all about this. How and why did you get yourself off your tiny island and all the way to Tuscany?"

Luciana took a sip from the steaming cup and then began to tell the story of what she'd been planning for months.

How she held no money, having no cause to ever pay for anything herself. That she did have credit cards but if she used them her whereabouts could be located. So she'd decided she would use a few precious stones to finance this expedition she was compelled to take. About how she carefully spread out on her bed all the palace jewels that had been worn by her mother, her grandmother, her great-grandmother and her lineage even before them.

Many were one-of-a-kind pieces crafted by the finest jewelry makers in the world and gifted to the royal family. Most of them were ornate and overdone, not at all pieces she would have chosen for herself. Yet she understood their legacy and importance. They would be passed down to her own children someday, either to a daughter or a daughter-in-law.

Returning those to the palace vaults, Luciana kept only a few plainer pieces whose stones would bring her enough money. They were everyday pieces that would never be missed.

The princess had also been keeping a careful watch on the schedule of supply boats that arrived regularly to bring goods onto the island. After reviewing her chart, she confirmed that one arrived at four o'clock every morning. Formulating her scheme, she'd creep outside the palace walls, avoiding security cameras and passing undetected through the pitch-dark of the wee hours to the shore. Finding a covering from which to spy, she'd timed the boatmen unloading their cargo and wheeling it through the service entrance of the palace. For at least ten minutes during the unloading process, the boat was unattended.

Gio put his elbows on the table between them, engrossed in her tale.

On the chosen night, Princess Luciana donned her darkest clothes, slid out the pre-packed suitcase from under her bed and placed the jewels into a purse. She left a note on her desk for her father, climbed over the terrace off her sitting room and scurried her way to the dock in the darkness. Once on the boat, she'd covered herself in tarps and sailcloth. Shuddering with fear as she heard the crew return to the boat, she'd all but held her breath as they pulled away from the shores of Izerote.

When the boat touched land in Barcelona, she'd waited for the crew to disembark and then, having no idea what would greet her once she was on deck, was able to dash away from the dock unnoticed. Although she didn't get the money she expected for the sale of the first jewel, she'd had enough to board a train, and transferred from one train to another to another through France until she'd reached Florence.

"I'm astonished," Gio said as he leaned back in his chair.

Replaying the getaway in her mind, Luciana was just as shocked as Gio that she had pulled it off. Not just the actual escape, which was something out of a spy story. But that she'd had the will and the courage to do it. To take something for herself that every cell in her body was starving for. That she would have spent a lifetime regretting it if she hadn't.

Maybe a little piece of this was also a tribute to her mother, who Luciana knew was never happy under the confines of her tiara. Her mother's eyes had died long before the car accident took her life.

"One question," Gio mused. "Why did you come to Florence for specifically three weeks? Do you turn into a pumpkin after that?"

"Worse. I'm getting married."

"You're set to marry a man you don't love?"

"I must wed King Agustin of Menocita, an island near ours. It's my duty to my subjects. Izerote is a land of unspoiled green hills and clear blue waters. But our population has been shrinking over the last couple of generations. With globalization, the people of Izerote want more in their lives than what our island has to offer. Families send their children off to the great universities of Europe and the United States where technology is up-to-date and there are job opportunities."

Gio raked a hand through his curls as he listened attentively. They nursed the cups of tea he had prepared. He'd met a couple of royals in his life at social functions but never with any intimacy other than a handshake. He did remember that he got a standoffish vibe from them, as if they were separate from the rest of the world. Princess Luciana, Luci, was not like that at all, and from her he sensed a benevolence he almost never felt with anyone. If he hadn't known, he might indeed believe that she spent her days as a teacher among the needs and simple concerns of toddlers.

"How is it that marrying King Agustin will be good for your subjects?"

"Menocita was heading toward the same fate as Izerote until about thirty years ago when Agustin's father decided the island would become a tourist destination in order to create jobs and attract visitors. And it worked well. They built lavish beach resorts and all the ensuing industries, which have brought prosperity to the island. Although now their waters are polluted and they have to ship garbage out by the boatloads."

"King Agustin and your father want to do the same in Izerote."

"Yes." Luciana took a demure sip from her cup of tea. Those sensual bow-shaped lips had held him captive as she told him her story. He loved her upright posture as she sat on the chair opposite him while they talked. The moon glow, plus a couple of garden lights, cast perfect shadows of light and dark across her stunning face. She'd worn a simple dark green dress to dinner tonight, very modest with its high neckline and below-the-knee length. Last night for the dinner with his investors, it was a stiff-fabric light blue dress, quite formal. He wondered if princesses were ever allowed to dress in casual clothes.

Really, though, it was the sight of her in that sheer nightgown on the Juliet balcony this morning that he couldn't get off his mind. It made him want to run barefoot through a forest with her, crown or not.

"Agustin's wife died when they were quite young. He must remarry and bear children."

"You're being traded for a couple of hotels on the beach?"

Luciana laughed out loud, the dulcet tones carrying into the foggy air of the late night. "Yes." She continued to giggle so sincerely, it made Gio smile. "I love the way you phrased that."

"It's true."

"And what's sadder," Luciana added with a snicker, "is that I dislike Agustin, what little I know of him. He's stern and humorless."

Princess Luciana was not like any of the women he'd known before. First of all, with Grasstech's position as the world leader in its field, Giovanni Grassi and Dante Grassi were two eligible bachelors of accomplishment and wealth. With that, they attracted women who tried to glam onto them for a taste of the luxury life. That's exactly what Her Royal Highness Princess Luciana was running away from.

Many a woman like Francesca had crossed Gio's path. Dante's, too. The women who gravitated toward the Grassi brothers were nothing like their mother, the down-to-earth woman who was grateful for all of the blessings she and their family had. Noemi Grassi didn't have a phony bone in her body, and raised her sons to be the same.

Yet Gio and Dante were magnets for women who pretended they were one thing but were really another. Francesca being the state-of-the-art, and most costly, example. After her deception, Gio made a firm decision never to trust a woman ever again. It was ironic that now he was sitting across from a woman most definitely out to deceive, yet her reasoning was understandable. And he appreciated that she had come clean to him. In a strange way, now he thought of himself as her confidant. Partner in crime.

"I do have to marry him. The wedding is set. Invitations were sent long ago. The dinner menu has been selected. An ugly dress has been created. In fact, it was that horrible dress that pushed me into this trip. Once I saw myself all bound up in that lace like it was ropes of bondage, I decided it was now or never to claim something for myself."

"What if you didn't go back after the three weeks?"

"I have to. I owe it to my father. I'll be surprised if I even get the three weeks. I don't doubt that he has already contacted palace security and blueprints are being drawn up as to how to find me."

Gio winced when he thought of how that must be for her. Essentially a prisoner of her crown. Not permitted to be the schoolteacher she said she wanted to be. Not able to choose who, and if, she wanted for her husband. Bound by obligation to put the throne first, and herself second.

"How would anyone find you after that careful escape you executed?"

"You have no idea the lengths my father would go to." Luciana licked her top lip. "But in my letter to him I promised that I would stay safe and return, and remain in service to our people all the days of my life."

Gio would be in service to his family for the rest of his life, too. Although not unwillingly. However, he would have preferred to stay in the vocation that he loved. To create new products, to get lost in the mathematics, in the scientific discovery of hypothesis and proof. Now he would stand as the voice and face of the Grasstech empire. Analyze operations. Maintain a dedicated and productive staff. Make decisions about expansions and new territories. He would do it, with authority and justice, even if he had a tad of reluctance. Whatever his family needed, he would deliver.

While Luciana had an arranged union that she was loathe to undertake but must, Gio would trudge his road alone. In his parents, he witnessed the kind of love and partnership that dreams were made of. His parents were romantic, with genuine well-wishes and support for each other every day of their lives. Most important, they were friends who trusted each other completely. Gio never expected to see any of that in his lifetime.

Yet for reasons he didn't quite grasp, it bothered Gio that Luciana belonged to another. No one should be forced to live out their days with someone they didn't love. It was wrong.

Gio's phone buzzed in his pocket. He read Samuele's text out loud. "Not a decent hotel room to be had, with several large business conventions in town."

Luciana's face fell.

"Why don't you stay here while you are in Florence? You see I have room." What else could he do but take her in? If this was to be her one big hurrah before a life devoted to what others wanted for her, the least he could do was watch over her and try to keep her safe. Yes, because she was a princess. Yes, because she was a sheltered young woman who might not know how to avoid the menaces that anyone faced when traveling alone. And yes, because there was something special about her that had touched his heart.

Of course it didn't make sense, his urge to take her into his arms and kiss away any past and future. To bear her burdens. To take away everything other than this courtyard and the moon and the moment.

"And I can show you around a bit." Getting off the computer and out among the human race would be good for him. And would make him a better leader, too. He needed to take the long view of his well-being now that he was the company's CEO.

Gio didn't know what was prompting him to get so involved in this young woman's trip to Florence. Maybe it was only that he spent so much time alone, it was a breath of fresh air to talk and walk with Luciana. And he sensed that she needed him. Which felt strangely good. But after learning the hard way from Francesca that he couldn't trust anyone, it was essential not to get close. There was something so virtuous and sweet-natured about Luciana, it would be easy to forget that vow. Fortunately, she'd be in his life for only a short time.

"Hello, Viggo." Gio's driver met Luciana in front of the villa. After he'd secured her into the car and pulled away she asked, "Where are we going?"

"Signor Gio asked me to leave it as a surprise."

When Luciana had woken up this morning and stepped out onto the Juliet balcony of her room, Gio was nowhere to be seen. Which she had to admit was more than a little disappointing. The day before, she'd relished such a lovely breakfast with her handsome host. She was hoping for a repeat.

From the balcony, she had looked down on the courtyard and eyed a tray set with a coffee thermos and what looked like a plate of food under a cloth napkin. After a shower, she dressed and made her way downstairs.

Upon closer inspection of the tray, Luciana found that it also held a single pink rose in a vase. Which made her heart skip a beat. She'd been given hundreds of elaborate flower arrangements and bouquets, whether at ceremonial processionals or formal introductions or sent to the palace. Yet she couldn't think of a flower she'd seen in her life that was as charming as that one rose on her breakfast tray. Because she knew it had come from Gio, and the mere fact that he had thought to include it brought a swell to her chest.

It wasn't merely out of respect for her title that he'd had the thought. Was it simply the gesture of a man who was innately hospitable? Or a man who appreciated the beauty of nature and thought to adorn the tray with a stem picked from the villa's garden? Or was it something else entirely? A time-honored gentlemanly practice of a man giving a flower to a woman as an act of romance?

Surprising herself with that thought, Luciana swallowed hard as she touched the velvety petals of the rose. Gio wasn't wooing her. And romance was never in the picture for Princess Luciana de la Isla de Izerote. Her parents and grandparents, and all the royal couples throughout Izerote's history, were beholden to the monarchy. Each and every one of the marriages had been carefully considered during meetings around a table between the male elders.

Some of the women in her lineage got lucky. Stories were passed down about her great-grandmother meeting her great-grandfather. At first, they clashed. He was a traditional man who concerned himself with laws and war. Whereas her great-grandmother was a nurturer, wanting to improve the lives of the poorest citizens of the island and a great lover of animals. It seemed they'd have nothing in common, and her great-grandmother grew quite sad.

Within a few years, three children were born. Luciana's great-grandfather fell in love with his children and their carefree pursuits of play and pleasure. Through those children, he and her great-grandmother fell in love with each other, some six years after they walked down the aisle at their wedding to each other as complete strangers.

It was important for Luciana to hope for the best. Maybe she'd find a camaraderie with Agustin. Or she'd uncover a good side of him. They might even become friends. She doubted she'd fall in love like her great-grandmother had in her arranged marriage. But romantic love wasn't necessary. The merger between the two islands was what mattered.

Luciana pulled back the napkin on the tray to see the same breakfast of rolls and fruit that she and Gio had lingered over the day before.

She thought of her grandmother and mother. They hadn't fared as well as her great-grandmother in their marriages to domineering men who did not allow their wives any independence or private pursuits. She remembered her mother's blank stare, that of a woman who was only going through the motions of her day. Although she knew her mother had loved her for the eleven years they'd shared together, even as a young girl Luciana could sense that something was wrong. Her mother fulfilled her obligations, but the deep corrosive peeling in her gut was too high a price to pay.

Harsh King Agustin had already informed Luciana that he expected her to begin producing heirs immediately and, in as many words, told her that a condition of his agreement with her father was the promise of her complete obedience. The thought of reporting to him as a servant was repulsive. Hopefully, in time, he'd come to see her more as a partner.

He would never set her heart on fire. Agustin would never on a whim present his wife with a single pink rose. Still, they'd find a coexistence she would come to terms with.

Luciana lifted the rose out of the vase and brought it to her nose to fully immerse herself in its lovely scent, the sweetness of the gesture and, most important, the man who had presented it to her. How they had sat here last night drinking herbal tea until the wee hours. She'd shared the story of her journey after assuming that she'd never tell it, that it would be a secret she'd take to her grave. Gio was so easy to talk to and listened attentively to everything she said rather than simply waiting for her to go silent so that he could resume talking like all of the other men she knew. They talked and talked and talked until they could barely keep their heads up.

After revealing her true identity to him, she assumed he would want her to leave his villa. Instead, after the shock, he seemed to understand her predicament. The backward ways of Izerote infuriated him. He was willing in his own small way to aid her on her voyage of discovery by offering her a safe haven.

Frankly overwhelmed by the incidents with the jewelry and the boys chasing after her and the lack of available hotel rooms, his kindly invitation was a relief she gratefully agreed to.

There was one other matter, too. The idea of spending time in Florence with a handsome, intelligent and freethinking man was simply too exciting to pass up. What a thrilling ride this had already become!

As she sat down to eat her breakfast, she wondered what time Gio had left this morning, as it was still early. He'd left a note.

Viggo will pick you up at five o'clock to meet me for more of your sightseeing tour. Casual dress.
Until then, Gio.

Now as Luciana was being driven through the streets of Florence to meet him, she kept replaying that *until then* salutation on the note. There was something incredibly alluring about those words.

She spent the entire ride trying to talk herself out of those thoughts. Certainly there would never be anything amorous between her and Gio. It was just an isolated girl's fantasies starting to spin out of control. She was about to be married, she was in Florence for three weeks and Gio was going through a transition, as well. He'd already declared that he was single and planned on staying that way. She felt guilty and wrong even having those thoughts about him.

But Gio had no idea what he'd done. Last night, she had satisfied a years-old yearning to visit the Piazza della Signoria, to sit in that storied square in the evening air. A scene she never could have imagined she'd be sharing with a man. One like him, no less. With his imposing six-foot-three-inch height and slim muscular build. The most bewitching eyes, blue as the midday sky. And that fascinating tousle of blond curls that she could convince herself wanted to have her fingers thread through them. Something she knew wasn't the case and wouldn't be in a million years.

Although it was nothing she could have planned, the evening was infinitesimally better in his company. Unfortunately, it was an evening so perfect it made her wish. And there was no place for wishes in the life of Her Royal Highness Princess Luciana de la Isla de Izerote.

Viggo pulled the car over to the curb and

Gio appeared to open her door and hold out an arm for her to take hold of. *"Buonasera."*

"Where are we going?" Luciana eagerly inquired, not used to surprises. That was another part of life as a princess. There was no spontaneity. Ever. A royal's life was plotted and protected from any intrusion that might throw off the organization. Plans were very important. People had to be notified, schedules had to be coordinated, itineraries had to be created. This rigidity was, of course, necessary to keep the palace running smoothly. "Your driver wouldn't tell me."

"Tonight, I'll show you one of my favorite pleasures from my adolescence. After dinner, we'll walk along the Arno River."

Luciana looked down at her dress shoes. They were made for appearances at children's charities, not for treading the streets of an ancient city.

Observing her hesitation, he said, "In my note, I suggested that you dress casual."

"This is as casual as I get." In fact, when the princess assessed the few outfits she had brought in search of the least formal, the best she'd come up with was a skirt that hit her midcalf paired with a lightweight jacket.

After nicking a suitcase for the trip from the palace storage room, she'd filled it with the only clothes she had. Dresses that were suitable for diplomatic luncheons and others for garden brunches. A few cocktail dresses for dinner. Luciana did not even own one pair of slacks. A princess worth her salt would never be caught wearing them.

"I see," Gio said as his mind shuffled through a thought.

"I'm curious about you." She gestured at his outfit. "This is the second time I've seen you in a jacket and tie with jeans. That's acceptable in your business?"

"I own fine bespoke suits. But yes, I work in jeans."

Obviously, she couldn't mention just how good he looked in said ensemble. This was a man who had a personal style and didn't care what anyone thought of it. He was unlike anyone she'd ever met before.

"I think we ought to buy you some jeans right now."

"Oh, no, I couldn't."

"So you'd stow away on a boat in the middle of the night, sell your family's jewels, sleep on trains to get to Italy, but you won't wear a pair of jeans?"

They both laughed. For Luciana, it was laugh or cry, and she'd done her fair share of the latter.

"You're an interesting study in contradictions," Gio pressed on. "Come on, I know of a shop near here."

He was going to take her shopping for casual clothes? Appearances were a big deal to royalty. They weren't supposed to look like commoners. The strict manner of dress garnered respect. She was again wearing the blond wig disguise, half assuming that operatives of her father were searching for her. The hair was enough of a change.

Yet she wasn't representing Izerote here in Florence. No one knew who she was other than Gio. Her heart began to beat double time. Walking the streets of Florence, both of them in jeans like a typical couple on a holiday? Simple denim was taking on a larger meaning. Maybe she really was pulling off the one thing she thought she'd never be entitled to. To know, just for a short moment in time.

Freedom.

Gio crooked his arm like he had last night, encouraging her to follow where he led. Silvery flashes almost dizzied her as she slipped her arm into his, opening her palm flat against the taut muscles of his biceps.

"Let's go, Princess."

CHAPTER FOUR

"I'VE NEVER BEEN in a shop like this," Luciana gushed when she and Gio stepped in off the street. Pinching herself, because she was surely living out a fantasy, in a busy boutique that sold everyday clothes to Florentine women, not tourists. It was as if she had inhabited someone else's body.

"You've never been to a clothing shop?"

"Not like this. Clothes are generally sent to the palace. Occasionally, we go to Paris or Milan to visit a designer's atelier. The building is cleared out and, of course, I'm accompanied by style associates, palace dressers and at least three bodyguards. I don't think I've ever in my life trolled through a rack of clothes on a sales floor."

"Have at it, Princess."

"Can I ask you a favor?" she whispered.

"Certainly."

"Will you call me Luci, like you did when

I first introduced myself to you? I'm sure it's not anything anyone else would understand, but I love the idea of just having a regular first name without all of the pomp."

Gio's eyes smiled into hers, producing a hot whoosh that flowed right through her. It wasn't a sensation she was familiar with and, frankly, it was terrifying. Of all things, what she most wanted to do was kiss him. Right on that gorgeous mouth of his. She'd never kissed a man on the lips. Nor was she going to now, but apparently when in Florence in the company of the most unexpected of tour guides, a girl could imagine almost anything.

"Shop, Luci." Had he somehow read her thoughts, because he redirected her to their purpose in the store? He knew as well as she did that they could never kiss. Ever since she'd met him a mere two days ago, she'd already had to mentally repeat to herself a hundred times that this extraordinary man had landed in her life, but that it would be for only three weeks and then never again. She was about to be married and that was that.

Now, to the matter at hand.

Luci surveyed the shop in action. The customers were mostly women, a few with bored men obediently accompanying them. A couple of the women combed the racks with great seriousness, methodically considering every item as they moved down the aisle. Perhaps they were on the hunt for something in a particular size or color. That was another thing Luciana had never practiced, as the size and color of her clothes were always preselected for her.

Some of the shoppers had items draped over one arm as they worked through the offerings with their other. Another behavior Luciana had never known. Servants and handmaidens were always at the ready in the princess's life, lest she ever have the need to lift a finger.

The store carried a range from what she assumed would be office attire, to resort wear, to casual clothes.

"There are the jeans." Gio looked up from his phone and pointed her to a display case that held dozens of pairs folded onto shelves. He tugged her by the hand and led her to the assortment. One stack held the darkest of blues, azure as the midnight ocean. Others were a lighter wash. Others still had tears at the knees, a lived-in look that Luciana had never really understood when she saw it on fashion websites. The jeans styles were listed, as well. There was boot cut, straight leg, skinny and something called boyfriend.

With Gio holding her hand, seeing the word *boyfriend* spelled out in front of her made her lungs drain of air.

"Everything okay?" Gio perceived the change in her face.

"Actually, I don't think I should do this. I'm only here temporarily. I can make do with what I brought."

"Don't you want some comfortable clothes to explore the city in? If you're concerned about the cost, I accept diamonds."

This time his humor was not well received, as Princess Luciana was beginning to feel very uneasy. "I'm not comfortable doing this."

"Your subjects aren't here. No one knows you in Florence. Didn't you say you'd always wanted to wear a pair of jeans?"

As she'd told Gio on the walk to the shop, she'd had one meeting with a pair of jeans. A princess from a neighboring island, one with less old-fashioned ways, had come to Izerote to attend a diplomatic function. Luciana explained her predicament and begged the other princess to leave the pair of jeans she had brought along. Within twenty-four hours, a palace housekeeper had found the jeans in Luciana's closet, assumed that a laborer had accidentally left them behind and promptly discarded them. Luciana never even had a chance to put them on.

"I suppose I could try a pair on."

"That's right."

"What do you think boyfriend jeans are?"

Gio summoned over a saleswoman who explained the relaxed fit of the boyfriend cut. While he tended to business, she assisted Luciana in finding a couple of sizes that were likely to fit, and showed her into the changing room. It was yet another first for her to take off her clothes alongside other shoppers, each woman separated only by a privacy curtain.

She knew perfectly well that both girls and women the world over would have their own fantasies fulfilled if they got to try on Princess Luciana's ball gowns and tiaras. Yet the sound of metal against metal that the zipper made as Luciana pulled up the jeans gave her a special joy. Biting her lip, she allowed her eyes to slowly move up toward the mirror until she could get a good view of herself.

Wow. For the first time she could ever recall, she saw herself as just a young woman. Who might have borrowed her boyfriend's jeans, which fit loose around the hips and seat as they were intended to. She loved the heaviness of the denim, understanding why jeans were popularized by cowboys and miners.

But she couldn't traipse all over Florence in jeans! They were too unceremonious. Even if no one else knew she was a princess, she'd know. About to take them off and at least treasure the memory of being in this shop on this day, she decided to show them to Gio.

"Luci!" Gio nodded his approval as she exited the dressing room to model for him. She knew there wasn't anything particularly flattering about the jeans, but she wanted him to see her like a normal girl, wanted to keep them on for just a little bit longer. *"Bravissima."*

"Do they look good?" she asked in a quiet voice.

"Turn around."

Turn around? Gio Grassi, tech wizard and almost complete stranger, had just ordered Her Royal Highness Princess Luciana de la Isla de Izerote to circle around in a pair of jeans so he could examine her behind in them?

But that didn't stop her from obeying his command. And deriving a wicked satisfaction from doing so.

"Well?" she challenged.

"You look like a city girl on the go. What do *you* think?"

"They're so comfortable. And the fabric is

so weighty. It makes me feel like…like my own person."

"We'll buy two pairs. You'll need tops and shoes, as well."

"No. I can't. It's not right. Trying them on was enough."

The princess glanced outside through the store window and noticed that there were two men in black suits standing near the entrance. Both wore earpieces that they spoke into. For a moment, she panicked that they were palace security from Izerote. That her father had already located her whereabouts and she was moments from being whisked back home.

If that was to happen, she steeled herself, darned if she wasn't going to first do some of what she came to Florence for.

"Thank you, Gio. I would love to buy these clothes."

"And don't worry. You're not getting anything for free. When we go to dinner, I'm going to need you to earn your keep."

Gio was happy to see that the rooftop restaurant he remembered atop a five-story building along the Arno River was still in business. With a view of the river and its many bridges, including the famous Ponte Vecchio, the trattoria was one of those secret-treasure restaurants that Florentines hoped no tourist would ever discover. Thankfully, it remained a low-key family establishment with an easygoing dress code.

Because now Her Royal Highness Princess Luciana, who had looked so dignified in the silken dinner dresses she'd worn the last two nights, was unfussy and relaxed in her new jeans, flat shoes and a T-shirt. She fit in fine with the young mothers out with girlfriends, and city workers, who unwound from their busy days with a glass of prosecco at the restaurant. Surely, no one would mistake her for nobility.

"Oh, my. This view is splendid."

As Gio took it in, he agreed. The red-roofed buildings, one after the next, lined the banks of the river and its stone bridges. Firenze was truly like nowhere else. Although it did occur to him that the sight of Luciana's face, with the sweet mouth and enthusiastic eyes as she took in the vista, was as stunning as the view itself.

At the office, he'd spent the day swamped with work. And could have put in several more hours. So he'd almost regretted having promised to take Luciana out tonight. Even though he had offered, he didn't really have time to play tour guide and rearrange his schedule. This was why he shouldn't spend time alone with women. The pheromones, or whatever it was they gave off, clouded his judgment. And he had a feeling that Luciana's pheromones had particular powers.

It had been entertaining helping her shop for those jeans. He shared her agony in buying them, though, knowing they represented more than a bit of cloth to her. In fact, his jaw tensed at the fact that something as simple as selecting her own clothes was an exception to her, not the norm.

The river glistened below as twilight was beginning to sweep the sky above, the open air taking on darkness. This was Gio's third dinner with Luciana. Considering he hadn't had dinner alone with a woman even once in the past few months, that was quite a record.

Lately, he'd been spending time immersed in development of some new biometric products. Generally when mealtimes rolled around he would ask for something to be brought in, as he was far too engrossed in his work to be bothered with leaving his desk. Or the whole team would go out for a late-night meal where beers and spicy food were eagerly consumed amid plenty of noise and clamor. He had no objection to either, although Luciana's lips, which appeared so pink in the softness of dusk, made him doubt that more pleasing company had ever existed.

Gio ordered wine and nibbles.

"You mentioned needing my help," Luciana said as she tore her eyes away from the river.

"Yes. I appreciated the suggestion you gave me about writing that press statement. To sandwich the hacking incident in between more positive news about the business. I hope the net effect was to put the matter in perspective."

"Do you think it did?"

"Somewhat. But the tech world is calling for details about the hack. Although fortunately no metadata was leaked, top secret information was breached. As leaders in the field, Grasstech always comes forward with information that could assist the entire industry."

"So you want to reveal more about what happened?"

Even though Luciana was involved in her own kind of deception, he held no ill feelings toward her like he did for Francesca, who'd misled him for her own personal gain.

Still, he had to remember never to tell Luciana anything truly confidential.

"Grasstech's advisers are pushing for this idea that I do an interview with the leading computer industry security magazine and talk about the hack from a strictly technological standpoint."

"Getting out in front of it rather than having the press snoop around is probably a good idea."

"And I have a live-stream chat scheduled with the computer science department at a local university. As you noted about my daily uniform—" he gestured down the length of his chest and then leg "—sitting bent over a computer all day, I don't give much thought to what I'm wearing. I put on a tie as a nod to my authority."

An appetizing plate of grilled vegetables and another of cheeses was delivered to the table. Both Luciana and Gio reached for a morsel.

"Are you suggesting we switch roles now? You've put me in jeans and now you want my help becoming camera ready?"

"Exactly."

"Ironic."

She smiled one of her bashful grins, as if she was sharing a joke only with herself. He supposed that the last thing she'd expected to be doing in Florence was giving public relations lessons to a techie billionaire.

"I'm all ears."

"All right, I've got an easy one for you. Take the jacket you have on right now, for example." She pointed to the blazer he wore tonight atop his starched shirt and Milanese tie. "Button it."

Gio followed her instructions.

"Now sit up very straight. Then reach behind you and tug down at the waist so that the shoulders stiffen back farther than they normally would."

Again, he did as she suggested.

Luciana approved.

"Now you have sharp, crisp lines. Very authoritative. And you can get the photographer or assistant to clip the jacket in back so it stays that way."

"I'll use that. Thank you."

This was a competent, and even confident, young woman. What a shame that her position wouldn't allow her to pursue whatever ambition she had. Gio could hardly imagine being held back intellectually. That might be a fate worse than death. Fortunately with the encouragement of his loving parents, he'd found the calling he loved in the computer sciences. Even if he had to turn to more administrative matters, he would still keep his hand in the product design he was so apt at.

"Could we have cappuccinos?" Luci asked.

"Certainly." Gio chuckled. The princess wanted a cappuccino while most of the women he'd ever known wanted far more. His money. Or his reputation. Or his secrets.

"What's funny?"

For an instant he looked at the woman sitting across from him as Luci, whom he was out with for an ordinary dinner date like many others around them in the restaurant. Where people came to talk about their days, or the tomorrows ahead of them. Where they didn't just eat a meal, but shared a human experience. They connected.

Would he ever make space for a personal life? His constant travel had been a deterrent to any long-term liaison. That was how he professed to want it, but was that really true? Or was he hiding from having to learn how to share himself with another, how to meet the demands of a relationship without diminishing his work?

There had been women here and there. If he was being honest, it was only to satiate bodily desires. Then he met Francesca. And became transfixed by her prowess of tech smarts combined with the looks of a film noir movie star from the 1940s in her dark clothes and red lips. Not unlike those old movies, it turned out she was a spy in disguise.

Gio had been duped. Perhaps his childhood was too idyllic, with parents who taught him to value honesty and candor. Trust. It was what he expected of others. Which proved to be a mistake he'd never make twice.

Peering left to right, he knew that no one in the restaurant would have any idea that Luciana was a princess. So while his pretty dinner companion had revealed her true identity to him, she still attempted to fool the city of Florence and Gio would remember a hard-learned lesson. Never let anyone get to him again.

After their delicious dinner, Luciana and Gio took a long walk along the banks of the Arno. He told her the name of each of the bridges that linked the two sides of the city. As they walked over the Ponte alla Carraia, they stopped to lean over the parapet and could make out the outlines of their reflections in the glistening waters.

They were silent for a spell in the glow of the night, after a dinner filled with interesting conversation. About the possibilities of technology. About the advances in communication, scientific research and the globalization of business. But also about the dangers of piracy and impostors on social media. The sharing of ideas made Luciana think of the great minds that had passed through this city over the centuries.

Although Her Royal Highness often sat in on meetings where matters such as improving the technology on the island were discussed, she was rarely asked her opinion. Plus, the conferences never motivated her father to take any action, and the island remained hopelessly behind the rest of the world. She wished futilely that she could bring some of Gio's heightened thinking and know-how back with her when she returned. But she'd be far too busy regrouping from her trip here, begging her father's forgiveness and marching toward her wedding day.

Still leaning over the side of the bridge, Luciana judged her image reflected in the water. She was wearing the straight blond shoulder-length wig that disguised her long and thick brown curls. Between the hair and the jeans—and, of course, Gio—her time in Florence couldn't be more different from what it was on the island. She recalled a cute expression she'd read in a magazine: people referring to a situation with the acronym YOLO. *You only live once.*

After listening to the quiet swish of the

river in the dark of night, Luciana was ready to talk some more.

"You're so lucky that you developed that genuine interest in technology without your parents forcing you to follow into the company if you didn't want to."

"I am at that. My parents told Dante and I that they'd never want to sell the business but that if we decided to pursue something else, they'd let others run Grasstech."

"Your parents sound like wise people."

"You say you'd like to be a teacher. Why aren't you allowed any vocation outside of the monarchy? Plenty of members of royal families have careers."

"None of the women in my family have, and my father won't permit it. For heaven's sake, I'm not even supposed to be wearing jeans!"

She couldn't blame everything on her father. Always wanting to please him and not cause him any more pain after her mother died, Luciana had often kept her mouth shut when she should have spoken up. And so outdated customs perpetuated.

"I couldn't bear the lack of liberty."

"This is the only existence I've ever known. I don't mean to sound critical. Of course, to be royalty is an unparalleled honor and I have many experiences few other people do. It's just that all we ever do in Izerote, really, is walk in place. I fear the world is passing my people by."

"Hence, the tourism that your fiancé will bring."

Luciana cringed at hearing Gio say the word *fiancé*. Somehow it sounded even more undesirable coming out of *his* mouth.

The princess had never been allowed to date. If she had, Gio was exactly the type of man she would have gravitated toward. An intellectual. An iconoclast. Someone without walls to his imagination. Who was determined, and knew how to achieve his goals. A man who was receptive, fair, considerate and could have a laugh at the world.

What was she doing? She didn't even really know this man and suddenly she was able to list his attributes? *While you're at it, Luci, don't forget drop-dead sexy!*

In fantasy, she could envision him as the perfect man and even make him hers. But in real life, he could be in a relationship. Married, even. He could have a girlfriend, a wife and even children in Hong Kong or Mumbai or any of the other places he mentioned working from recently. Perhaps they were waiting for him to get everything settled in Florence before he sent for them.

Somehow, she didn't think so. It sounded as if he'd come to distrust the people around him. Probably even more so after that hack. As a matter of fact, he could be running some kind of charade of his own and she'd never be the wiser. She'd be smart not to forget that Gio Grassi was merely an unexpected addition to what was already a dream, but definitely one that she would wake up from.

Once again, she had to remind herself to remain optimistic about her future. Duty had its own rewards even if it was sometimes hard to see it that way.

Gio gently nudged her arm with his elbow, sensing that sadness was beginning to take her over. She half smiled in return.

"It won't be so bad," he said softly. "It sounds as if you love children. Even if you can't be a teacher, at least you will soon have some of your own."

"Yes, but what will I be birthing them into? The isolation of the palace?"

"They'll have you. You'll teach them to understand a larger world."

Luciana's eyes blinked back tears. Everything Gio said was so supportive. And she was so aware of not wanting to give the impression that she was ungrateful. Yet she burned inside for more to her life. To challenge her brain, to stretch her soul, even to explore her body.

There was a wedding night to come when her virginity would be taken for the purpose of breeding. Yet she knew that marital relations could involve more than the obligation to her monarchy.

From reading novels and watching movies, she could fathom carnal longings. She'd had vibrations in her body that hinted at pleasure, that even promised ecstasy. The way her breath had stuttered when Gio had placed his palm on the small of her back as he'd ushered her into the restaurant this evening. The way he always offered the crook of his arm for her to take, which forced her body to brush against his, making her swoon a bit each time.

She'd implored herself to shut down those reactions to him. They were highly improper.

However, the battle was being lost.

Standing on the bridge with him right now, she could hardly contain herself. She wanted him to grab hold of her, to take her into his arms with a male urgency that was savage. That knew her not as a princess but as a woman made of flesh and blood.

Not willing to settle any longer for only

the reflection of him in the river's water, she turned to face him and he followed suit. She gazed into his eyes that shone like stars in the night.

As if reading her mind, he bent down toward her face and softly kissed her lips. His touch might have been light but a thousand sensations shimmered down her body, waking every inch of her.

Not willing to stop there, she stood up on her tiptoes to bring her lips to his a second time. She felt her softness melt against his firm mouth to share another stolen kiss. Knowing that she should back away, she instead opened her mouth slightly, to know the kind of kiss she'd read about in books and seen in movies. A lover's kiss, only for him. Which joined them and made her wish it was forever.

Her knees went weak.

As hard as it was, she finally pulled apart from him.

He reached to twirl a lock of her hair in his hand. And then abruptly let it drop from his fingers. "I forgot you were wearing a wig."

"It looks real but it's artificial to the touch."

"I shouldn't have kissed you. I'm terribly sorry."

"I wanted you to. I kissed you in return."

They looked at each other in anticipation. Of what? "It can't happen again."

"I know."

Their eyes locked for what might have been minutes or it might have been hours.

Finally, they had to break their gaze and returned to looking down into the river.

"Do you dislike my wig?"

"I'll admit I was shocked when you removed it to show me your natural hair."

"It's as if I'm someone else when I wear it." Someone who would kiss a man she was so attracted to she might have burst out of her skin if she didn't. "I like it."

"You should keep wearing it, then, Luci. You should do whatever you want to do."

Those were words Luciana heard so seldom she could hardly make sense of them. Do what she wanted to do? Right now what she was dying to do was to kiss this amazing man again. In this most romantic of places. Under the dark skies and atop this ancient bridge.

However, she'd settle for wearing the new clothes and the wig, playing a game of reverse dress-up.

And she'd savor having heard Gio utter words she never expected to hear.

You should do whatever you want to do.

CHAPTER FIVE

PRINCESS LUCIANA LINGERED across the street from the hair salon for the longest time. Watching the activity, she observed as women entered through its heavy glass door. Other women exited, and Luciana found herself imagining what their hair might have looked like earlier that morning. How many were just getting a trim of the style they had been wearing for a long time, a hairdo that their family and friends and coworkers were quite used to? Or were some experimenting with entirely new haircuts and colors, reinventing themselves from the hair down? Would they go home to compliments from their partners, or would their kids make fun of Mommy's new look?

Were the women leaving the shop happy with their new hair, or would they look in the mirror later in the day and bemoan that they had made a terrible mistake? Would they seek consolation from their sister or best friend, who would convince them that it would grow out soon enough?

Luciana thought she could stand there all day and contemplate the women of Florence, their lives and their loves. And their hair.

Luci would dash across the street, bound through the salon door and declare exactly how she wanted her hair done. Luciana wasn't so bold. When she did finally cross the street, it was slow and tentative, half of her not believing that her arm was actually pulling the handle of the door. In one fell swoop she opened it, hunching over a bit so that no one would see as she quickly yanked the blond wig off her head and stuffed it into her jacket pocket. Her own long curls fell down all around her face.

"May I help you?" a receptionist at the front desk greeted her. She'd obviously not seen the princess's slick move to remove her wig. The dark-haired woman, with a pen in one hand and a phone in the arch of her shoulder, juggled many activities.

"I'd like to get a haircut and color," Luciana murmured tentatively above the pounding electronic music and echoing chatter in the modern shop. It was designed with beige furnishings and bamboo trees presumably to give it a Zen sort of look that was totally incongruous with the decibel level of noise.

"Say it again, sweetheart," the receptionist requested.

"Cut and color, please," Luciana said a little louder.

"I have Gabriel available."

The woman pushed a button on a console. Luciana flipped through one of the hairstyle books on the counter and chose a photo of a cut that looked exactly like the wig she'd been wearing. Within a few minutes a slim young man with bleached white hair and many bracelets on one arm approached. Luci thought him very fashionable and excitedly told her inner Luciana not to be frightened. This was a good idea.

"*Carina!* Gorgeous face," Gabriel said as he took Luciana by the hand and brought her to his salon chair, fourth in the line of eight along the long wall. The chairs were white leather with a silver-studded pattern around the edges that, ironically, made them resemble thrones. A bite to the lip helped Luci hold back a giggle. Each throne faced a large mirror and shelves that held combs, scissors and other tools of the trade. "Take a seat. We'll talk before we cut."

"That's a relief."

Gabriel lifted her mane of hair and wove it in his fingers. "Healthy. Thick and glossy. But kind of like a child, long without a style, right?"

"Yes!" Luci exclaimed. "I have had my long hair as it is for my entire life." Just as her mother had worn her own long hair. Natural, perhaps brushed back from her face with a headband or arranged to complement a tiara.

"We need something modern," Gabriel said as he examined all of Luciana's hair, "and chic, right?"

"I'll show you," she piped up and showed him the photo from the salon book. "This."

"Blond. Shoulder length. Yes, this will look splendid on you." With a quick sweep, he gathered up all Her Royal Highness Princess Luciana's hair and grasped it in one hand. With the other, he reached for a pair of scissors from his workstation and held them in the air. "Are you ready?"

"Yes," Luci answered for Luciana, who was speechless and terrified.

"I'll take off some of the length and then we'll truly begin."

"Do it," Luci eagerly agreed in anticipation. Luciana clenched both her teeth and her fists.

With just a couple of snips, Gabriel cut a good six inches from the length of hair and let it fall from his hands. He and Luci and Luciana all watched as it hit the black salon floor.

Luciana's mouth dropped open in shock.

"Can I offer you a coffee?" Gabriel asked.

"Absolutely," she answered without hesitation.

As Gabriel worked his ministrations on her locks, Luciana reflected on how this trip had turned into much more than what she bargained for. Not only was she cutting her hair and wearing pants and touring Florence at her leisure, something far more important had happened. A six-foot-three-inch something, to be exact.

Jeans fade and hairstyles grow out, but meeting Gio would linger with her for the rest of her days. Last night on the bridge was surely the most romantic interlude she could possibly conceive of. The way they watched each other's reflection in the water. How they turned to stare into each other's eyes. Then he'd kissed her. What's more, she'd kissed him back. A real kiss!

Which they'd immediately backed away from. Both understanding that nothing more could ever happen between them. Knowing that what already had happened was too much.

They'd stood in the courtyard of the villa

when they'd returned from the river, neither of them wanting to go to bed. In that prolonged good-night, a piece of Luciana died. She'd realized the totality of what she would never have. This swirling dream she was dancing in could last for a few weeks, but that's all it would ever be, a milky vision to reflect back on like a photo in a memory album. That was all she'd be taking home with her.

Sleep had eluded her. It was too grand not to recall over and over again their walk along the banks of the river. The way they chatted and discoursed, even argued, about everything they could think of from politics to art history to the evolution of Grasstech. Gio's family was so progressive. They thought far and wide. They took bold chances and weren't afraid to fail.

Princess Luciana wished she'd grown up with people like that around her. Her mother had been, effectively, silenced long before she gave birth to a daughter. While in her heart she had the utmost respect for her father's decisions to preserve Izerote's natural beauty and its idyllic way of life, that wasn't what Luciana would have chosen for herself.

"*Finito,*" Gabriel chirped with a flourish as he lifted a hand mirror to show Luciana the finished job. Luci smiled from ear to ear because it looked exactly as the wig did, but now it was hers. It belonged to her. She could float up on angel wings for her hair felt as light as a feather without the weight of its former length down her back. The color was dramatic and sophisticated. Luci complimented Luciana on looking like a self-assured young woman, no longer a little girl.

Thankfully, Gio had insisted on giving her some money to keep in her pocket, so she was able to pay for the salon services.

Gio said he'd take a lunchtime break to show her one of Florence's most visited sights, the original statue of *David* at the Galleria dell'Accademia. Viggo would pick her up in front of the villa soon. She decided to wander in what was essentially *her* neighborhood now. A bench at a small park beckoned, where she took in the noonday sun, let the rays shine through her new hair and replayed the electrifying kissing from last night.

A child's ball hit her on the leg and snapped her out of her meditations.

"Mi dispiace," a tiny voice apologized as a little boy came to fetch the ball. Probably about four years old, he had dark corkscrew curls and huge black velvet eyes.

"That's okay. Here you go." Luciana rolled the orange ball back to the boy, who wasn't able to stop it. It passed behind him. The child stood only a few feet from the bench Luciana was sitting on and she had rolled it very slowly on the ground, so it was odd that he had missed it.

"Matteo!" A woman about Luciana's age retrieved the ball and brought it back to the boy. "Try again, bambino." The boy took the ball from her and ran toward the other six or so children in the park.

"Hi, I'm Luci. Do you care for all of them?" Luciana asked the woman.

"I'm Chiara and I suppose you could say that. I'm their teacher." She pointed to a small building attached to a church. "We've come out from the nursery school to play before the children take a nap."

Luciana watched the children, who were now chasing pigeons. She smiled at their lovely faces.

"Do you enjoy being a teacher?" she asked the young woman, whose hair was piled into a loose bun and who wore an airy blouse with a lot of stains on it. Probably everything from paint to clay to jam.

Her Royal Highness often made appearances at schools and children's charities in Izerote. Of course, when she toured a facility she was dressed as a princess and rarely given anything to do but meet the children, who stared at her as if she worked for Disney. Or she might be permitted to do a nonmessy craft with them for five minutes. Nonetheless, she treasured the visits.

While there, she might observe a particular quirk about a child. How one interacted socially, perhaps having trouble when another child was around, or crying at the slightest provocation. How much she wished she could formally study the behavior of children, to play a part in helping them grow up to be fully functioning adults.

"Of course, Luci." Chiara brushed some dirt from her own hands while her eyes never left the children. "To encourage the evolving young minds, to listen to their ideas. What could be better? What do *you* do?"

Obviously, she couldn't reply that she was a princess. "I'm finding my way," she answered wistfully. "I'd love to work with children."

The two women conversed a bit more, both keeping a vigilant eye on the needs of the children. As Chiara had just expressed, to watch each child interact during play held endless fascination for Luciana. While at university, she'd taken classes in child development, but how she longed to earn an advanced degree. To study different styles of learning, gender analysis, social conduct. To make a difference in the lives of precious, unrestrained children.

For a fleeting minute, Luciana felt like Luci, a denizen of this great city. A woman who had a direction and was at ease with herself, and who was in a secure relationship with a wonderful man.

What? Luciana caught her own thought. Even if she were free to love, Gio had made very clear that a serious relationship was most definitely not on his agenda. Last night's spontaneous kisses had probably meant nothing to him. Not only did he need to concentrate on the responsibilities of running an enormous corporation that was on top of its competitors, Gio was a man who lived out of a suitcase without entanglements. Just because he was spending time in Florence didn't mean that was immediately going to change.

Nonetheless, for just an iota longer, Luciana pictured her life as a Florentine schoolteacher in love. Imagining what she was going to cook for her man tonight and the warm embraces she'd have with him in their bed.

The boy with the big doe eyes threw the ball to Luciana again. She tossed it gently back and, again, he missed it.

"Chiara." Luciana leaned in toward her so the boy wouldn't hear. "I don't think he's seeing the ball clearly. Has he had his vision checked? I think he might need eyeglasses."

"That's a good observation, Luci. I will mention it to his parents when they come to pick him up."

After Chiara and the children left, Luci walked home to get ready to sightsee with Gio. Feeling very Luci indeed.

Although Luciana kept insisting that she wanted to see Florence as a typical tourist would, Gio was sure she'd just as soon not queue up for hours to see Michelangelo's *David* at the Accademia. Nor did he have the time to do so. Therefore, he was glad he had asked an assistant to book tickets in advance for a reserved entrance time. As it was he'd had to rearrange several meetings in order to free his schedule for a few hours. It was actually rather ridiculous that he was sightseeing in the middle of the day.

Gio himself hadn't seen what was one of the most visited locations in Europe in many years. He'd forgotten just how imposing and magnificent *David* really was until they approached the statue, ringed by tourists studying the work from all perspectives. The marble champion, who as the story went, was a young shepherd when he slew his powerful opponent, Goliath, with cleverness rather than might, stood raised on a pedestal for all to see.

"Michelangelo was only in his twenties when he carved this," Luciana commented to Gio while they both studied the details. "What an amazing achievement for such a young person."

"In addition to all of the other works he did in his career."

"One of the greatest artists the world has ever known. I've been waiting for so long to see this. Thank you for bringing me here."

"Look at how defined the eye sockets are. That gives him such a look of watchfulness."

"That's what they say about the biblical character it's based on. David has his slingshot there—" she pointed to the detail over his left shoulder "—that he used to defeat Goliath with only five stones."

They moved incrementally around the statue, carved from a single block of marble, observing every minute feature. The prominent veins in David's hands, the rigidity of his muscles, yet his bent left leg suggested the innocence of youth. The work was so well preserved and compelling that it felt as current now as it had been when Michelangelo created it in the early 1500s.

Gio felt himself relaxing. There had been a couple of stressful moments already today when he'd had to make decisions related to the employee structure of the company. People's jobs were on the line and it was up to him, and ultimately only him, to decree what was in the corporation's best interest. Which could be a ruthless job. He'd called his father at the vineyard. They'd discussed it over the phone and come to a decision.

He was especially interested in deciding on a new location for a manufacturing plant to produce his new slate of biometric products. With the dozens and dozens of offices and manufacturing sites Grasstech had amassed, Gio enjoyed bringing new and good-paying jobs to towns or villages whose citizens needed the employment.

"Do we have time to see some of the other works of art here?" Luciana asked after they'd circled David three times.

"I'm all yours."

Luciana looked at him with big eyes as a small smile fought to come across her mouth even though she resisted it with a bite to her lower lip.

Gio fought a grin, too, at the words that

had come out wrong. He was hardly all hers, for heaven's sake!

Last night as they'd stood on the bridge, he didn't know what had driven him to kiss her, a move he hadn't been planning and knew he mustn't repeat. But there hadn't been a glimmer of censorship as his head bent down for that split second of contact with lips as pillow-soft as could be. Most unexpectedly, she'd lifted them to kiss him again and hadn't settled for the brief brush he had. No, she'd kissed him like a lover, bold and self-assured. With that, she'd rocked him to his very core.

After they'd lingered in the villa courtyard and finally said good-night, he'd lain awake in bed, high on Luciana. Like she was a drug that sent him levitating above his body. She was like no one he'd ever met, exhilarating and tragic all at once. Thoughts of seeing her again had popped into his head all night long in spite of his telling himself to get to sleep.

Gio had spent so much time alone. Even before the fiasco with Francesca, he'd been only casually dating, never able to see how a woman would fit into his life. A life dedicated to his mind and to creativity would be it for him.

Like many people who entered the world of computer science, he was not especially social by nature. More comfortable inside technology, absorbed in work. Like Michelangelo, who was said to sometimes lie down on the ground in his clothes and boots to sleep in small increments because he worked almost continually and barely ate. Gio understood how it was to get lost in a project, in the painstaking process of solving one problem after the next until he developed a solution.

Even with his parents' nearly sublime marriage as an example, Gio never imagined himself as someone who would settle down with a wife and children. He feared because of the attention he paid to his work that he would never be able to give a family the focus they deserved. Yet spending time with Luciana, it dawned on him that, with the right person, anything was possible.

"I want to see the slaves." Luciana brought him from his musings.

Taking her by the hand, and registering its smallness in his, he snaked through the crowd and led her to another hall in the gallery that held the works usually referred to as the *Prisoners*.

Four of them were on display here and others in museums elsewhere in the world. These Michelangelo works were considered *nonfinito*, or incomplete, although it wasn't known for sure as to whether he had left them unfinished on purpose as a way of explaining his own artistry.

"Michelangelo was quoted as saying something to the effect that he was merely a tool and that the sculptures were already there in the marble. His job was only to carve away what would allow the art to be seen," Luciana said.

"Ah, so we both studied art history at university. It was a good counterbalance for me to the world of science and mathematics."

"I've always been especially drawn to the Italian masters."

The four works were devastating. Each depicted a man who had not yet broken through and was still trapped within the marble. With a leg or a torso or a face not yet visible, they appeared to be half man and half stone.

"Some scholars speculate they represent man's struggle to be free," Luciana added pensively. Her face changed from admiration at the work to something personal and melancholy. Gio guessed it was the idea of being trapped in marble, bound, incomplete, unable to actualize one's full self, that had gotten to her on a profound level.

Out of the corner of his eye, Gio spotted two men wearing black suits who appeared to be looking their way. They didn't hold professional cameras or else he might have suspected that they were paparazzi that recognized Princess Luciana, although she'd told him that she was not a high-profile royal like some. Anyway, with that blond wig she was so enamored of and her new wardrobe of comfortable clothes, he doubted that the press would make the connection.

He dearly hoped that they weren't palace security from Izerote, a possibility that Luciana feared. That her father had been keeping tabs on her all along. That perhaps an arrangement had been made to allow Luciana a couple of days under the delusion that she was on her own when, really, she'd been surveilled by her father's missives all along. Who might pounce on her any minute, thereby ending this expedition that meant so much to her.

Although he was sure he would have detected it previously if they were being followed. Subtly glancing over to the men again, he saw they were now turned away from Gio and Luciana. Perhaps they were just undercover overseers for the gallery.

Strangely, he wanted to protect the princess. Fury bubbled in him as he watched her study the captives in marble, knowing she was in her own prison. Fury at her father and at a faraway land he didn't know, for forcing her to conform to outmoded conventions and gender rules that made no sense to Gio. If only he knew of a way to help Luciana's island of Izerote so that she didn't have to marry the neighboring king.

Why he'd come to care so much about Luciana in such a short time, he didn't know. Maybe it was his general disdain for injustice.

After Luciana had her fill of seeing a few of the other halls of art in the Accademia, they exited. "I can afford a little more time. Let me show you another tourist sight. Did you change something about your wig? It looks nice."

"This is the Ponte Vecchio." Gio swept his arm across the vista of the bridge filled with people.

"It's much different from the ones we saw last night." Luciana studied the bridge that was lined on both sides by shops and structures with windows.

"Centuries ago, it was butchers and fishmongers who sold their wares along this bridge. Now, as you can see, there are galleries and souvenir shops but mainly jewelers."

Indeed, Luciana and Gio walked past one small jewelry shop after the next. Gold, silver and other precious metals beckoned from the outward-facing glass cases the vendors used to attract buyers. Gemstones sparkled. Tourists pointed at items.

"It's an old saying that many a man lost his fortune by taking his wife walking along the Ponte Vecchio," Gio declared.

They observed as a man and a shopkeeper excitedly argued, their arm gestures and shaking heads indicating they had not yet reached a deal. A group of young women pointed at diamond rings from another vendor. Every few storefronts, instead of fine jewels, tables of figurines depicting the statue of *David* were for sale. Little *Davids* meant to sit on a desk as a memento of time spent in Florence. Naked *Davids* on cell phone cases. Luciana smiled wryly. Had she been princess of a larger monarchy, she might have ended up with her own likeness on a coffee mug.

From the bridge, they stopped to watch a sightseeing boat as it made its way underneath.

Gio bent his arm for Luciana to take, and they continued on.

A necklace caught Luciana's eye. Simple silver, its several strands of different lengths created a statement.

"Do you like that?" Gio inquired why she had fixated on that one piece.

"It's only that I have one very much like it."

"Did you sell it in Barcelona?"

"Not that one."

Suddenly, guilt thundered through Luciana's body. Had she completely lost her mind, selling palace jewels? Which technically didn't really belong to her. They were only hers to wear during her reign and would then be gracing her children and their children and so on. What right had she had to sell what wasn't even hers?

Her heartbeat sped to a rapid thump. In coming here, she'd rebelled against her father, who only wished for her protection. He was probably worried sick. If only he would have been more lenient with her, had let her travel, and had encouraged her to study and explore her curiosities. Or if she'd been more defiant, rather than always placating him. Then maybe she wouldn't have gone behind his back to take this drastic action most unfitting to her position. He must be in shock after his obedient daughter, who always thought first of pleasing him, had fled the island just weeks before her wedding! Yet she'd never meant to hurt him.

Absentmindedly, she touched her hair, still

surprised by how silky and lightweight it was. Even Gio had complimented her on it today, without knowing why. She'd chosen not to tell Gio about the haircut. Not wanting him to think she'd taken on yet another form of disguise. It occurred to her that with his wealth and status, women left and right must present themselves in ways they think would attract him, whether it was their true selves or not.

Now she thought of her new hair as just another disappointment for her father. It would grow out. Just like the haircut, this crazy adventure would be a blip on her radar. Once she returned home, she'd take her rightful place. This city, the statue of *David*, Gio, would become pale remembrances that were completely incongruous with the life she was to lead.

Perhaps someday she'd return to Florence, to show her children the superlative art or to appear at an official occasion. She'd arrive on a private plane to be met by a limousine, and with bodyguards and palace personnel surrounding her like a butterfly net, she'd be escorted from one building into another. Never breathing fresh air, never strolling the backstreets, never watching children play ball in a park.

And she'd most certainly never, ever keep

company with this fascinating and accomplished man who made her see herself as anything but a sequestered dusty relic on an island that no one cared about.

"You're regretting your decision to have sold some of your jewelry?" Gio leaned his head down close to hers as she fixed her gaze on the silver necklace.

"I don't know if I should have come here. I think I've made a terrible mistake."

"You won't regret this. It will help you along your path."

She looked him in the eye. "Why are you such a wise old sage for a techie?"

Gio laughed, a resounding guffaw that bounced through her, making her visualize yet again what it would be like to be married to a man with whom she could talk about big concepts and laugh with a dark sense of humor.

"You've learned about me already, *bellissima.* I have a mind for profound thoughts and no common sense in other matters. Which reminds me, I wanted to ask your opinion about the press statement for our new facility in Dallas."

Along the Ponte Vecchio, they chatted about catchphrases and wording. Luciana was grateful she had knowledge about *some-*

thing that was useful to him. Dealing with the media was a valuable thing her father had taught her, to be careful what she said and did because someone was always watching.

Her arm in Gio's, they sauntered on. She willed the yearning that rose when her body brushed against him to subside. There was no reason to think Gio had those same stirrings in return. He was not looking for love, and would not accept finding it, either. She sensed he'd been hurt by love, although he never went into any detail about it. That kiss between them had been spontaneous, and it was she who prolonged it. Nothing was going to change between them as a result of it.

Which was perfectly okay. In fact, it was essential. He could be relied on to keep her growing emotions in check. Because hers were moving into dangerous waters.

"I really do have to return to the office," he said, "but I'd like to share with you one other important thing that both locals and tourists do after they've been exploring our city's streets."

"What is that?"

"Let me show you."

They reached the opposite end of the Ponte Vecchio. The bridge emptied out to the Oltrarno, the other side of the river, the part of the city that had many historic places to see but was much less touristy.

Her arm in his, Luciana had a feeling she would follow him anywhere. He took her down one quiet street and then made a right into another and another until she thought they were secret agents outwitting evil foes.

With this little dash into the Oltrarno, he had brought them far from the crowds, from the doggy dishes with pictures of *David* on them, and the salt and pepper shakers shaped like the Duomo.

Finally, they reached their destination. Gelateria dei Frediano.

"Gelato, Princess. All the problems of the world could be solved with the right gelato."

He held the door open for her to enter the shop. The smell of fresh cream immediately took her by storm. Patrons sat on ice cream parlor chairs around small marble tables, giving the place a historic vibe. In fact, there was a sign above the old-fashioned cash register that read Established 1929.

Luciana eagerly inspected the cold cases that held silver trays of many flavors of gelato in small batches. From the caramel color to the pale green to the chocolate-studded white, each one promised to be more delicious than the next.

"How could one ever select?" Luciana exclaimed, glancing up to Gio, who had been watching her as she deliberated at the glass cases.

"Pick several. We'll have a tasting menu."

"They all look delectable. You choose."

"Why don't you have a seat over there?" He pointed to an empty table in the far back of the shop.

After a few minutes, Gio joined her with a tray of three small silver dishes, all containing scoops of the creamy treat.

"What did you get?"

"I'll let you guess," Gio said as he sat down and placed the tray on the marble table. "Close your eyes."

"What?"

"Close your eyes so that you can focus only on the taste of the gelato."

She was both entranced and horrified at the suggestions that she should close her eyes here in a public place. But she knew that Luci would think it was fun to shut out the distraction of sight so that she could become intoxicated by the flavors. For her sake, Luciana obliged.

With her eyes closed, she was hyperaware of Gio's presence next to her. Warmth and strength emanated from his direction.

Was he going to kiss her?

After a moment of almost unbearable anticipation, the first thing she sensed was the cold metal of a spoon as it touched her lips. Gio maneuvered the spoon a little bit so that it coaxed her lips to part. "That's right," he murmured softly, his voice crawling over her and making her twitch in her seat.

She felt the first bit of the gelato move from the spoon into her mouth. The pure creaminess coupled with the sweet flavoring made her tongue circle. "Oh," she moaned after the first of it slid down her throat, "that was so good."

"What flavor do you think it was?" he asked but then didn't give her a chance to respond as he slipped another spoonful of the same flavor between her lips.

"It tastes like nuts," she answered in a voice that didn't even sound like her own. Did Gio know how much he was arousing her with his little game? That as he fed her the ice cream, a secret pulsing was starting from down inside her body, in her most intimate center? And that the sound of his voice was only making the throb pound stronger and louder?

"Nuts. Good guess. But what kind?"

To get any last bits that could help her formulate her answer, she rolled her tongue all the way around her lips to catch every drop. At that action, a whisper-quiet groan escaped from Gio's lips, causing her to open her eyes.

"No fair, Luci. Close your eyes," he ordered and she obeyed.

"Is it hazelnut?"

"Very good." He dabbed at her lips with a napkin, and her spine sharply straightened. She knew that no one in the shop would be able to see them, as the table was in a dark corner and Gio's back was shielding them from view. But she did momentarily consider how wholly inappropriate this exercise was.

It was only a fleeting thought, though, before the metal touched her lips again, making her forget who she was, what she was, as she could only surrender to Gio's spoon and what it told her to do.

"This one is easy. It has to be strawberry. The pink one I saw in the display case."

"You're good at this, Luci." They both knew why he kept mentioning her Florence nickname.

He ran the tip of the spoon along her lower lip. Her tongue followed the motion to chase any specks of the fruity goodness that might have lingered. Then he abruptly took the spoon away, and the tip of her tongue darted out to try to catch it, though it was gone. Gio's easy laugh shot straight into the base of her belly.

"Are you ready?" He brought the spoon back to tease her lips apart again. Her eyes involuntarily popped open. His smiling face and the nod he gave her was an unspoken direction to close them again. Which she did, with a slow inhale that filled her lungs with the fragrance of the shop.

To the next creamy offering, she rolled the gelato around her mouth again. "Chocolate. A dark chocolate at that."

"Taste more," he said as he fed her another bite.

"Delicious."

"Exquisite."

"Did you have some?"

"No. I was talking about..." He stopped himself.

Luci raised her eyelids. Gio wasn't smiling anymore. His brows creased and his nostrils flared. There was a flush in his cheeks.

"Is something wrong?"

"No," he bit out. "I need to get back to work."

In a split second, his mood had gone from playful to upset. She didn't understand what had happened, and truth be told, she was intoxicated from the ice cream feeding. His displeasure was making her dizzy.

He shot up and pulled her so she was standing, too. Then he steered her out of the shop so fast her feet didn't touch the ground. With a quick wave, he hailed a taxi and secured her inside. "I'll walk to my office from here and see you later at the villa."

CHAPTER SIX

"TELL HIM WE'LL ship the first hundred thousand to him by November." Gio gave Samuele his verdict during their daily briefing in his office. It was late afternoon and the sun had moved away from the windows, letting a thick whiteness blanket the sky.

"That's a reasonable commitment. But what is bothering you?" The older man leaned forward in his chair facing Gio at his desk. "You are snappy and distracted."

Why did Samuele have to read him so well? Maybe because he was like an uncle? Because he'd been with the company since the beginning? Had watched Gio and Dante grow from young children into men?

Gio gave him a snarl, though it was quickly diffused by Samuele's loving smile.

The truth was, Gio still hadn't recovered from that gelato-eating-turned-erotic encounter he'd had with Princess Luciana a few hours earlier. Not to mention the explosive kiss the night before. He reprimanded himself for his impulsive behavior. There was no way that spoon-feeding sweet ice cream into her luscious little mouth was going to have been a good idea. What he hadn't realized was just how bad a move it was. Because while he may have satiated Luciana's appetite for the Italian treat, it had left him ravenous. For her. Which was not in the plan at all.

Indeed, as he played the guessing game with her and her eyes had closed, a craving came over Gio so powerful it almost pushed him to madness. Watching her pink tongue dart out to chase the ice cream was a sight he couldn't imagine would ever get old. A voracious surge had forced itself through him as he told her to keep her eyes closed, leaving her defenseless and in his charge.

There was more he wanted from her as he visualized at least a dozen places on her body where he'd like to sample gelato from. By the time that list was made, the hunger was visible on his body, and he'd had to shift sideways in his chair to keep the princess from noticing. It was at the most inopportune moment that she opened her eyes and was able to perceive his discomfort with the arousal.

Gio studied Samuele's face, wrinkled with age but still very much alive and present.

"Samuele, do you trust Ginevra?" Samuele's second wife. His first had died young.

"Of course. Without trust there is no love. And without love, life is not worth living."

"But do you really trust her? Do you keep secrets from her, about work or about your hopes or feelings? Because you're worried that one day she might use something against you?"

"*Mio amico*, what are you talking about? Of course I've trusted both of my wives with everything. Just as your father trusts your mother."

Gio's telephone rang. "Yes. Schedule that meeting for two weeks."

"I understand. This is still about that woman in Hong Kong."

Francesca. Samuele had guessed correctly. Gio had no idea how to reconcile the disloyalty she had dealt him with the love that the men around him had for the women in their lives.

With casual encounters his norm, it had been fairly simple for Gio to make his decision after Francesca showed her true colors. That betrayal had put his company in jeopardy, his family in jeopardy. She'd been the only woman he'd ever let get close, and so he was convinced that was that. He'd never let a woman in ever again. Nor did he have any inclination to.

Sure, he could date all the women he wanted. A new one every night if he so desired. Without intimacy, without even good faith.

Ever.

Easy.

Over and done.

So why was he questioning that proclamation?

"When you meet the right woman, you'll know," Samuele continued. "It fits perfectly with your coming back to sit at this desk, doesn't it? Firenze is your home again, and she will find you here."

"I think you're wrong."

"Love has a way of showing up whether you think you're searching for it or not."

When Samuele left his office, Gio replayed his words over and over. Maybe love was meant to be for Samuele, who had the good fortune to find it again after loss. However, it wasn't going to happen for Gio.

One thing he was crystal clear about was that the mischief at the *gelateria* with the princess hadn't been a good turn of events.

For either of them. Whatever force had come over him while feeding the sweet ice cream into her scrumptious mouth needed to be locked back up, and quick.

It was probably another unwise plan that he told her they'd cook dinner together at the villa tonight, as they had been going to restaurants since the day she arrived. Being at home with her would be much too friendly. After he'd thought he might lift delicate Princess Luciana de la Isla de Izerote up onto the marble table at the *gelateria* and ravish her with a passion he didn't even know he had, spending the evening alone with her might be dangerous business he shouldn't dabble in.

But she was so excited when he'd told her he would come for her in time to visit the food stalls at the Mercato Centrale, he didn't want to let her down. It certainly wasn't her fault that his gentlemanly self-control was being tested to its limits. Technically, it was her fault for having such a swanlike neck and porcelain skin and caramel eyes as fine as the gelato she'd tasted. However, the internal struggle to keep himself from again pressing his mouth into those bowed lips was his, not hers.

If nothing else was able to hold him back,

there was one truth of such importance that it would supersede any other impulses he might need to fight.

He didn't know it as fact, but he'd make an assumption.

Her Royal Highness was almost certainly a virgin.

A virgin bride, soon to be married. No matter how much Luciana protested that she would never love the widower king she was to wed, Gio could never live with himself if she gave her maidenhood to a man she met on a prewedding runaway holiday. And, man-to-man, however unpleasantly she described her fiancé, Gio wouldn't carry on his shoulders any part of her deception to him.

A gruesome thought came over him. No one still utilized medieval methods of examination to ensure a princess bride's virginity, did they? He didn't know if indignities like that were even historically factual or just folklore he'd heard of, but that was another thing he surely didn't want to spend his life worrying about. Because, much as he hated to admit, he had a premonition that he'd wonder about Princess Luciana long after she left Florence. He'd best be careful to leave his fantasies at just that. Not realities he'd mull over for eternity, knowing he'd done the wrong thing.

It was simple, then. Under no circumstances would he let anything else romantic happen between him and Princess Luciana. Not tonight and not ever.

"Florence's central market," Gio announced to Luciana when they exited the car.

An enthusiastic smile crossed her lips.

"So many people." She flipped her head from left to her right.

"Yes, this is one of the busiest parts of the city."

The streets that surrounded the old market building were filled with outdoor traders selling their wares under tarped canopies to shelter from any weather. Buyers thronged three deep to peruse the offerings.

"Can we look at these stalls before we go into the market?"

"Of course."

"I've never been to a place like this before."

Gio didn't doubt it. While he had wandered through the souks of Morocco, the bazaars in Istanbul and the Far East Asian night markets, Luciana had no such experiences. Being in crowds such as this would be considered too dangerous for a princess to walk through.

Even with an entourage, he supposed the princess had probably never been in a crush of shoppers.

They maneuvered into the thick of the marketplace. Unlike the food and food-related products that dominated the *mercato*, the outdoor vendors sold leather, pottery, souvenirs, scarves and sunglasses. Each stall was attended to by a merchant or two, some yelling about their wares or special pricing.

Luciana was so aware of people all around her, her eyes darting this way or that when someone touched her.

"I'm not used to being so physically close to so many people."

"You're going to be bumped into, rubbed up against and even shoved. If you're uncomfortable, let's leave."

"Certainly not," she said, giving his hand a playful tug that brought a hitch to one corner of his mouth. "I'm not made of glass, you know. I won't break!"

Gio had a moment's caution when he thought of himself as responsible for her safety. Even though no one had put her under his supervision, he considered himself nonetheless to be her guardian. After all, she was a princess in a strange land.

Judging from the happiness on her face,

though, she was having too much fun to be daunted with any further warnings. Besides, while there were surely pickpockets and thieves in the area, the San Lorenzo markets of Firenze were hardly dangerous places. He'd watch over her to make sure she used common sense.

"Look at those colors." She pointed to one stall that held a selection of silk scarves hanging from hooks. Bright pinks and purples and yellows, every color in the rainbow was utilized in the dying of fabric to create them.

An emerald green scarf captured Luciana's attention. She looked around to see how other shoppers inspected the merchandise, unsure how close a scrutiny was customary.

"You can touch it," Gio prodded.

Luciana reached out to a corner of the scarf, rolling it between her fingers, then holding it up to check the transparency.

"One for fifteen, two for twenty-five." The hawk-like merchant quickly seized on her interest. He added a sales pitch, "The color is beautiful with your eyes."

Luciana let go of the scarf and they started to move to the next stall.

"Wait," the scarf vendor called out, "try it on. I'll give you a deal."

Gio and Luciana smiled at each other.

She glanced back at the scarf that she really seemed to like.

"Haggle with him," Gio said to her. "That's the way of these markets."

"I can't do that."

"Of course you can, Luci."

The green hue of the scarf was apparently enough to lure her back. The merchant detached the item from the dozens he exhibited on hooks. Luciana stepped closer and the man wrapped the long scarf twice around her neck, creating a very chic style. He handed her a mirror to see for herself. "I'll give you two for twenty, a special price, only for you."

"Do you see a second one you like?" Gio whispered in her earshot only.

She shook her head no.

"Then make him an offer."

"I only want one," Luciana stated to the merchant, but in a tentative voice.

"Usually I charge fifteen for one. I'm offering you two for twenty."

"No," she said with a firmer volume that made Gio proud. "If you'll give me two for twenty, then how about one for ten?"

"You'll have the other one for a gift," the vendor persisted.

When she returned to her home at the palace, Gio knew that Luciana was not going to be giving presents she'd bought at street markets. No, instead she would be spending weeks, if not months, trying to quell the anger of her father and her fiancé after she'd run away on this trip. Souvenirs were not going to be appropriate.

"Take the scarf off and hand it back to him," Gio counseled. "Then we start to walk away again."

The merchant grunted as she tried to hand him the scarf. "You drive a hard bargain, *bambolina*." He wouldn't take it from her, insisting that she hold on to it. "Okay. Thirteen-fifty for one."

Luciana shook her head. "Twelve."

"Twelve? You want to put me in the poorhouse?" he balked with a grin.

"Twelve," she said with resolve.

"Okay, okay."

Inside the old market building, as it had been for centuries, fresh food was for sale. As he and Luciana browsed the first aisle, several stands held the ripest-and juiciest-looking produce, from dark greens to crisp bell peppers to oranges with skin so bright you could almost smell them from a distance. Another stall had dried pastas in every imaginable shape, some tinged black from the ink of squids, others flecked with a beautiful green from spinach. A big wooden sign leading to a kitchen area read Pasta-Making Classes Here.

Another merchant sold a wide array of olive oils from regions all over the country, the amber of their color distinguishing the varieties. Yet another stand was lined with a case of fine cheeses, from the creamy and runny to the crumbly hard of the finest Parmesan.

"What would you like to cook tonight?" Gio asked Luciana as he enjoyed seeing the green scarf around her neck and recalled the negotiation for it with amusement.

"Perhaps pasta and vegetables? And cut fruit afterward."

"Pasta with a sauce?"

"Last night at that restaurant by the river we had simple pasta tossed in olive oil and fresh tomatoes with basil. Let's make that."

Luciana chose a seller she thought had the most enticing offerings.

"I've never picked tomatoes before," she confided to Gio. "I'm assuming they should be dark and firm."

Together, they chose tomatoes from a big pile, showing each other potential candidates for the other to approve. The stall was supervised by an old woman in a knit hat who probably assumed that he and Luciana were a couple. Although they could be merely co-workers, or even siblings, or just friends.

Friends? Was that what they were? Gio barely knew how to understand these last few days let alone put a label on them. Friends had to start from some point but soon knew each other well, often seeing one another through the trials and tribulations of their days. He and Luciana weren't that. They were friendly acquaintances, he'd grant only that much.

As he watched Luciana sort through the bunches of basil on offer, he contemplated whether she had hoped that romance would be part of her exploration here in Italy. Maybe she had longed to know attraction and lust before the arranged marriage she was to enter when she returned home. Maybe she'd imagined being swept off her feet by a swarthy and confident Italian Casanova, a stereotype perpetuated in movies and TV shows. He believed her to be virtuous, but he did wonder if she wanted to play at courtship in this most romantic of cities.

That was something he couldn't help her with. Too risky, for one thing, if his own body's reaction during the gelato tasting was any indication. And thank goodness she'd pulled away after that passionate kiss on the bridge. Gio wouldn't have the slightest notion how to pretend to woo a woman yet be expected to know exactly when to back off and put the charade down so that he kept it safe for her.

He wouldn't step foot in that territory. If he wanted something he took it, and nothing stopped him. Maybe he was that cliché of an Italian lover, after all. Because want Her Royal Highness he did, so he had to jerk back his own reins.

Luciana brought the tomatoes and basil to the old woman so that she could weigh them and charge her.

"Three-fifty," the woman said. Gio reached in his pocket for his cash and began to count it out.

"Three," Luciana challenged. The princess was apparently using her newly learned bargaining skills, not knowing that produce wasn't usually brought to auction.

"No, Luci," he said with a chuckle, "these are set prices."

After all the groceries were purchased, Gio and Luciana made their way out of the market and onto the street where Viggo was waiting to take them home.

In the car, Luciana scrunched her nose with concern. "I should have mentioned that I don't know how to cook."

"I've been living in hotels for years. I have no idea how to cook, either. But it's just pasta, right? How hard can it be?"

At the villa, Gio used his key fob to open the doors to the main residence of the villa. Since Luciana had been staying at the compound, she'd never been inside the *big house*, as he called it.

"So this is where you grew up?"

"Here, and summers at the vineyard." Gio had described the vineyard and winery in Chianti where his retired parents now lived.

As they stepped inside, Luciana admired the furnishings in the huge sitting room that faced the courtyard. Glass doors running the entire length allowed light, and fresh air if desired, to permeate the room. The space was divided into different sections. One sitting area was close to the doors, with two sofas facing each other and some armchairs. It was done with white and pink fabrics, giving it a cheerful mood.

A dining area with a long rustic wood table able to seat twenty or so took up another portion of the room. Comfortable-looking upholstered tan chairs surrounded it. A grouping of dark green chairs was arranged in a corner by a fireplace where tall bookcases lined the walls.

Everything was done in a casual sophistication befitting this most successful of Florentine families. It made her want to meet Gio's mother, whom he credited for the interior design. Large mirrors everywhere gave the room an ambience that was stately without being at all stuffy. Art objects of historical significance sat on side tables, and Italian landscape paintings adorned the walls.

This was distinguished yet unceremonious. Stylish without taking itself too seriously. Comfortable in its own skin yet at the ready to summon strong passions.

Oh, wait. Luciana was reviewing the furniture, not Gio.

She couldn't resist a long gander at his visage as she caught it in profile in one of the mirrors. There was no doubt he was a breathtaking man. Although because he was, at heart, a scientist with his nose in a laptop much of the time, he was hardly the entitled playboy billionaire one might expect based on his family's success.

He'd mentioned that there had been women in his life he viewed as predators. Luciana didn't doubt that there might be many who saw only money and position when they looked at him. Women who were motivated by what they could get from him, be it a luxury lifestyle or a career gain. That must be tied into his reasons for staying single, not letting anyone get too close. He'd probably experienced personal betrayal, been used.

For her, being with Gio made her actually believe in trust.

And hope. And enthusiasm.

And a womanliness she had never known anything of before. Never to be nurtured in her, but it was nice to know that it existed.

Or was it torture?

She'd been having the most daring thoughts, ones that the kiss on the bridge and the gelato tasting only served to heighten. Gio made her want to explore something that wouldn't be found in a travel book. Luci, too, had begun to wonder about…

Lovemaking.

With Gio.

Could that be part of her awakening here in Florence? To know the pleasures of the flesh? That kiss had prompted a flood of desire, as if it had been shored up inside her and only Gio could set it flowing.

"This way to the kitchen." Gio jogged her out of those visions as he carried in the grocery bags they had bought at the central market. Luciana touched the green scarf still wrapped loosely around her neck. She knew that slip of fabric was going to be ultimately tucked into a back corner of a drawer in her bureau at the palace. Years from now and decades after that, she'd pull out the testament to the prewedding journey that changed her view of life, and herself, forever.

Perhaps it would have been better not to have taken this trip. Then she'd never have to live with the memories of bargaining at the San Lorenzo market or of taking in the sheer brilliance of Michelangelo's *David*. Of watching joyous children play in a piazza. And especially of Gio awakening her sexuality and forcing her to understand want. In the end, she might even hate him for showing her something she could never have.

What if she didn't go home? What if she could just stay here with him, in this beautiful villa, for the rest of her life? Would that smash her relationship with her father beyond repair?

She'd always put her father first, thought long and hard against taking any action that might displease him. Perhaps she should have better understood her own yearnings all along, and learned to negotiate with him rather than simply obey. Maybe then her need to catch her breath away from the demands of the palace wouldn't have become so desperate. Might her father in time have come to accept that she could not live her entire life denying her hopes and aspirations?

"Oh, how nice," Luciana commented when they entered the kitchen, brightening to appreciate the moment at hand. A black-and-white-tiled floor surrounded a large island workstation. Hanging light fixtures contributed to the slightly 1950s retro look, everything painted white with some red accents. Several ovens, refrigerators and an industrial-style dishwasher let her know that this was a kitchen created for entertaining. Built-in cupboards and pantries attested to the smart design of the space. A large rack that hung from the ceiling held copper pots and pans and baskets of other cooking tools.

"My grandmother used to cook up a storm in here. When all the family was here for a Sunday supper or a holiday, we were a formidable crowd. She'd have every implement in use."

"On her own?"

"My grandmother cooked everything. Mom and my aunts would pitch in to get everything on platters and served. They always left the cleaning to the kids. They said they didn't want us to get spoiled rotten. That cleaning the kitchen, which would look like a tidal wave had hit it by the end of the meal, would be good for us."

"Was it?"

"Of course. It built teamwork among the cousins. Plus, it was a big job so it forced us to develop a plan, delegate work, problem solve. Fabulous training for anything in life, really."

"I'm never allowed in the palace kitchen. It is attended to around the clock by staff. It's too risky for me to be in there. After all, a fork might fall to the floor." Luciana spit out sarcasm that surprised even her. "If I ever want a tea or something other than at meal-times I, of course, merely press a button and it magically appears on a silver platter."

"Okay." Gio inventoried the ingredients he laid on the counter. "Spaghetti with diced tomatoes, basil, grated cheese and olive oil."

"Sounds wonderful."

"Why don't you wash the tomatoes?" he directed Luciana, who was only too delighted to have a task in the kitchen. She took note of the shiny skin and rich red color of the tomatoes they had picked. Turning on the tap at one of the small sinks, she rinsed their lovely selections and dried them on a nearby towel.

This was already great fun. She thought up a pretend scenario for her and Gio, preparing a simple weeknight supper just for the two of them. Perhaps they'd put the pasta into large bowls that they'd hold on their laps while they watched television. Both of them having changed from their workday clothes into loungewear, she'd wear striped fuzzy socks while Gio sat barefoot as they laughed at an American comedy show.

Never to be.

She watched as Gio filled a large pot with water. He carried it over to the stove and lit one of the burners under it.

"Right now, we can cut up the tomatoes and basil." He read the instructions on the spaghetti package. "When the water boils, we put the pasta in for eight minutes or until al dente."

"Why do you think it says *or* until al dente? Why wouldn't it be eight minutes every time?"

"Because the instructions don't indicate exactly how much water to use. It reads *'Fill a large pot with water.'* If you had two pots of boiling water but of differing volumes, that could affect the time it takes to cook the pasta."

"Okay. That makes sense."

"Also, it reads *'Boil over a high heat.'*

That's not very specific, as burners would vary from kitchen to kitchen. As a matter of fact, some are gas and some are electric, which would, theoretically, produce a different result."

About a half hour later, Gio and Luciana stared openmouthed at the sloppy mess on the stove. Splatters of tomato seeds and skins, and once-green basil leaves that had now turned black, dirtied the white marble countertop.

They peered into the colander that held their inedible meal.

"I wish my grandmother had taught me how to actually cook something." Gio shook his head in disbelief. "After all, it's chemistry. I should be good at it."

"What do you think went wrong?" Luciana lifted a slimy strand of spaghetti from the floor and then let it fall into the pile with the others.

"Maybe we shouldn't have put the tomatoes, basil and olive oil directly into the boiling pasta."

"I thought we would top it with the cheese."

"I have a hunch everything was intended to go over the cooked spaghetti. Nothing but the pasta was supposed to go in the boiling water."

"Ah, that's why the tomatoes exploded."

"Why didn't I look this up online?" Gio mashed his lips together.

"We thought it was going to be simple."

He brought over a small trash can, and used his hand to swipe some of the mess from the countertop into it. Luciana assisted by dumping the entire colander's worth of food into the trash, as well.

Next, Gio retrieved a couple of soapy sponges and together they cleaned up the disaster. Luciana had to admit to herself that even cleaning held a special satisfaction for her, as it was such an ordinary part of life for most people. Maybe King Agustin would allow her to take a cooking class if she expressed interest in it purely as a hobby. If he'd permit it, she'd be sure to pass anything she learned down to her children. Surely propriety of the throne wouldn't be compromised by young people learning how to cook an egg or a bowl of pasta!

Once they were done, the kitchen took on a hush.

"Now we need to figure out what to eat."

"I'm not that hungry after this afternoon's gelat…o." Luciana could barely get the word out as she was overwhelmed again by the recollection of Gio's sexiness with his game about the flavors.

Their eyes caught each other's for an extended moment. Longing bubbled out of her like an overly filled pot of boiling water would on the stove.

He picked up the one tomato they hadn't used for their fiasco. "Why don't we slice this tomato onto toast with a dot of olive oil?"

"Do you think we can handle that much food preparation?"

"Despite evidence to the contrary."

"Let's take it out to the courtyard."

There they sat close to each other, enjoying their beautiful tomato from one plate until all the stars came up in the sky.

"Your wig catches the moon's glow." Gio fixed on her blond locks. What he didn't know is that the hair he was admiring was real.

"Does it?"

"Let me show you," he said as he picked up a section to hold in front of her face. He realized that the texture felt different. "Wait a minute."

With his wide hand, he squeezed a cluster of her hair against her scalp. Expecting some movement from the wig atop her head. Nothing shifted. Another chunk, same result.

"I knew it didn't look the same as it did yesterday."

"I had my own hair cut and colored this morning to match the wig because I like it so much."

"I thought you said your father wouldn't approve."

"I don't care anymore."

"The tigress has been let out of captivity."

"You know," she said, licking her top lip, "it's you who are to blame. First you talk me into buying jeans, then you tell me I should wear my hair how I'd like to…"

Luci—it was definitely Luci—was unable to finish her sentence because without thinking about it first, she leaned over and kissed Gio's lips.

A groan exhaled through him and ricocheted to her, emboldening her to kiss him a second time.

He took hold of the back of her head and brought her closer toward him. Their mouths touched yet again, and with that, she was sure he set her on fire. They kissed more, his scorching lips pressing urgently into hers.

Flames licked at her legs under the table and quickly worked their way up her body. She had never been so fiery.

The contact of their tongues sent the blaze

upward to totally engulf her. As their kisses went longer, the moon stood still and Luciana willed daylight never to come.

Please let this moment last forever!

Both of Gio's hands traced her hair until they slid down to her shoulders. Which he took hold of and pulled her tight to him. When his lips traveled behind her ear and down her neck, she shuddered with uncontrollable pleasure. A moan she couldn't negate or retract came forth from deep within her.

A chill swept over her when he took an instant's break from the embrace. Yet it wasn't a bitter wind that put out the fire. Quite the opposite, the pause from his kisses only fanned the flames to make her want more.

Gio stood. Why? Where was he going? Her normal brain functions scrambled, not even processing her own questions.

"You are so difficult to resist." Gio raked both of his hands through his curls and took in a slow breath.

"Don't resist, Gio."

"There will be no turning back."

"Please."

With that, he reached down and picked her completely up off the chair and into his arms. Relief overtook her at the return of his touch.

Her arms wrapped around his neck as if it was the most natural motion in the world.

She couldn't have anticipated what was happening, nor deny the fact that it was what she wanted. Needed. Luciana tried feebly to protest, but Luci handily silenced her.

He brought her from the courtyard table to the front of his guest cottage. With an elbow, he bumped open the door and lifted her through the threshold. Once inside, the layout identical to her cottage next door, Gio carried her up the stairs and into his bed.

CHAPTER SEVEN

ALL GIO COULD concentrate on was the two kinds of comfort invading his senses. One was the calm presence of the morning sun through the bedroom windows, letting him know that he'd slept later than usual.

The other lay next to him in his king-size bed. Her Royal Highness Princess Luciana de la Isla de Izerote slept facing him, her exquisite features in repose without flaw. The blond hair she favored bathed her face in gold. If only he was an artist so he could capture her beauty this morning and preserve it for all eternity. Or if Michelangelo was still alive, Gio would commission him to carve Luciana's likeness into marble.

Actually, he might not need anything to help him remember this morning, as the recesses of his mind had already snapped pictures he'd treasure forever.

Gently, Gio brushed away a strand of hair

that fell from Luciana's forehead across her eye. She stirred the tiniest bit from his touch. The ever-so-small curl of her lips affected every inch of Gio's body, forcing his loins into an involuntary stretch.

With the mild temperature, he didn't perceive the need to pull the blanket over Luciana's alabaster shoulders. Instead, his eyes traced slowly downward to appreciate the curve of her breasts. He'd luxuriated for as long as he'd wanted to last night with the perfection of them in his hands, in his mouth. With his lips, his tongue, his teeth, he'd taken her entire body…

He'd done what?

Gio scratched his beard stubble as reality blew in the window. Late last night, after the disastrous attempt at cooking pasta and after they'd settled for tomato on toast and a humble table wine, the evening ended here. In his bedroom.

Where he took the virginity of a princess.

One who was engaged to be married.

Who was leaving Florence in a few weeks.

And whom he'd never see again.

It was hard to decide which of those truths was more disturbing.

Last night. With their laughter over their culinary foibles and her bargaining during their shopping expedition. Her cute yawn and outstretched arms as the evening got later. Finally her, no doubt, impulsive move to lean in and kiss him. He was unable to deny her. The faint voices in the back of his mind that had told him to be careful, to keep his distance, to remember that Luciana was to be a fleeting memory, had no strength last night. They went down without a fight.

All Gio had been able to hear was his own heart hammering in his chest and his gut stoking a fervor that couldn't be contained. It was the savage need that had been unshackled at the *gelateria* and never restrained, waiting, waiting, growing more powerful every hour. With every indication that it was what she wanted, too, taboos were cast aside as he carried her up the steps to his bedroom.

Her Royal Highness arched her back in her sleep and Gio's body firmed in response. Gazing at her, forgetting was easy. That she wouldn't be his. And how that was what he wanted. No love. No trust. Not to be depended on.

Why was the bravado of his credo fading further and further into the background?

"Good morning." Luciana opened her eyes and murmured a singsong.

"Good, indeed." Gio tickled a feather kiss onto her cheek and another to her bare shoulder.

Yes, ladies and gentlemen, Gio Grassi of world-renowned Grasstech had made love to a princess.

Those two starter kisses were not enough and he trailed another dozen down the length of her arm.

Their fusion last night had been a combination that shouldn't have worked, yet did. Primitive instincts had driven him while the purity in her eyes relied on him to go slowly, to measure her for pain or fear.

"Are you sure about this?" he'd asked once more.

"Yes, Gio, yes," she'd assured.

Relief swept across her face when he fitted on a condom. After that, soulful kisses and the sweetest of smiles informed the rest of the night. His satisfaction had been incomplete until he'd made certain that she'd experienced every pleasure a woman should know.

Eager to teach her more, he bent over to cover her face with a million kisses until the blankets were flung off the bed and the sun moved later into the day.

A lazy few hours later, Gio held Luciana in

his arms. "I've got to get to work. You, lovely miss, are bad for business."

Of course he was joking. Because, in reality, after making love with her he surged with energy and creativity. Ideas popped into his head about how to finalize the design for the new motherboard chipsets Grasstech was developing.

Funny how spending these days with Luciana hadn't been reducing his attention to his work but had been enhancing it.

As agonizing as it was, he separated himself from their embrace and got out of bed.

"*Bellissima*, do you want to help me with a magazine interview? That was part of our deal, wasn't it?"

She slid her fingers through her hair, visibly surprising herself with the feel of her new do, which she had apparently forgotten, causing Gio to laugh.

"Only if you'll take me to see more sights later."

"You're coming to the office with me."

"I am?"

"Up and out." He pointed toward her guest cottage. "Go get dressed."

After he heard her pad down the stairs and out the door, he stepped into a hot shower. For a minute he regretted not inviting her to join him, as the travertine shower was easily an ample size for two. But he really did need to get to work, and Luciana plus a steamy shower plus a bar of fragrant soap was not going to add up to getting him out of the house anytime soon.

They reunited in the courtyard. Viggo was outside and quickly ferried them to Grasstech headquarters.

"We'll go in through the back, shall we? I have a private entrance to my office. Better that the staff doesn't have something to gossip about."

"Absolutely, thank you. I appreciate that."

Her eyes were a bit glazed and something about her didn't look as princess-proper as she usually did. Gio bit back the craving that threatened when he realized that the change was due to the girl who had now blossomed into a woman.

In his office, he slid one of his small desks to face opposite his large one. That way, he could easily work with her on the interview while he mapped out the design for the chipset.

Several hours passed in a most pleasant fashion. Gio not only liked glancing up from his computer to find Luciana opposite him, but she was really quite helpful assisting him in how to phrase his answers to the interview questions.

Despite the unalterable fact that she was going to be returning to Izerote, Gio's mind wandered in a direction it shouldn't have. He speculated on what it might be like to see Luciana every day.

In her perfect world, she'd be a teacher so she wouldn't be sharing an office with him. But perhaps in the mornings, after they made love and learned how to prepare breakfast, Viggo would drop her off at school on the way to Gio's office. On days when he didn't have meetings, he could meet her for her lunch break. And after the long day had passed, they'd rush home to each other's arms, where they'd stay entwined until the morning light arose once again.

There was nothing about that fantasy that had anything to do with reality. He was just daydreaming because he hadn't wanted to be with a woman this much in…well…he couldn't think of a time.

"Do you want to say something about the origin of the hacking incident?" she asked.

He was finally ready to share with Luciana the detail he'd withheld. "I'm not going public with this information, but the hacker was a woman I dated." If that's how it could be categorized. Dated. More like worked and slept with. There were no candlelight dinners or tickets for the theater.

"Oh." Luciana looked up from the laptop with raised eyebrows. "I don't know why I assumed it was a man."

"In grungy black clothes surrounded by computers in a dark basement, right?"

"Something like that."

"I was fooled, too."

There wasn't much more to say on the topic. It was a humiliation he'd have to live with. But it was something he'd wanted to tell Luciana. Then he busied himself with other matters.

When the sun set over the city, Luciana asked him, "So, tour guide. Where are you taking me?"

He'd already thought that through. And he'd also come to the conclusion that he had every right to enjoy himself with this delightful woman. Circumstances were such that it was never meant to be more than a fleeting affair. A coming-of-age for Luciana. Why shouldn't he bask in her company while she was here and leave it at that? He'd had short-term flings with women before. He knew how to do that. When the goodbyes came, he and Luciana would part knowing that for that short time one autumn in Florence, two people were good to each other.

So why was it his heart had a hard time believing it would be easy to let her go?

"We're going back to the *mercato*?" Luciana inquired when Viggo dropped off her and Gio at the now familiar sight. Recognizing the old market building and the outdoor stalls where she had bargained for that green scarf, she knew exactly where they were.

"Follow me." Gio took her by the hand and maneuvered through the people heading this way and that. Entering the food market, they reached the stand where they had bought the pasta that they'd managed to render inedible. Gio walked her past the sign she remembered from last time: Pasta-Making Classes Here.

Through a doorway was a small commercial kitchen. Work counters were wedged in wherever they would fit. A pink-cheeked woman in a chef's coat welcomed them. "I am Chef Katia. You are here for the class?"

Gio provided her with his name, which she checked off from a clipboard she held in her hand.

"We're taking a cooking class?" Giddiness wiggled through Luciana. With her father considering the domestic arts irrelevant to royalty, and her and Gio's culinary debacle last night, if there was ever a person who needed a cooking class it was her. How thoughtful of Gio to plan this activity.

Speaking of activities, she was still in shock about the one she'd participated in last night. She blamed Luci for talking Her Royal Highness Princess Luciana into it, but nonetheless, it was clear to her from the first kiss that she was going to make love with Gio. She'd had to experience the hunger and intensity and ecstasy that two people could share. Need insisted she act with abandon, wildness even, and to learn the profound strength of her femaleness and her sexuality.

For all she might have hoped the intimacy would bring, it was infinitely more divine than anything she could have ever have imagined.

It was hard to picture leaving Gio now. She felt so close to him in a way she'd never have thought possible. He'd even confided in her that the company hack that caused him so much anguish was of his own doing in trusting a woman who'd systematically figured out how to work through him to get what she wanted.

The pieces fit together. How suspicious he'd been of Luciana when she'd first run into him on the street after those boys harassed her. And how he'd said that some women he'd known were predators. This one, Francesca, had really got the best of him. It was utterly horrible that she'd pretended to genuinely care for him when, really, she was out for personal gain. His work and his designs meant so much to him, there could be almost no worse betrayal than to steal that. No wonder he'd resigned to stay single.

How would it play out if she didn't go back to Izerote? Would Gio come to trust again? She envisioned a life filled with freedom and peace where they could go anywhere, do everything, be anything. As long as they had each other, nothing could harm them. Would he take that leap of faith if it was offered?

"If everyone will take a place, we will begin." Chef Katia called the class to attention and pointed to the stations she had set up on the worktables. Each area had a wooden board, bowls of flour and eggs, rolling pins, towels and other accessories.

Gio and Luciana took spaces next to each other as the chef began her instruction.

"We'll make a mound of flour and then dig a well into the center of it." Glee filled Luciana as she burrowed her hands into the flour. She loved the cool, powdery texture of it through her fingers. "Into the center, we'll crack the eggs."

Neither she nor Gio knew how to properly

crack an egg and both struggled, with giggles, to remove the shells that weren't part of the recipe. Chef Katia came over and demonstrated her technique. On the second egg, both Gio and Luciana shocked themselves by performing perfectly.

After forking through the eggs as instructed, the chef taught them how to gradually incorporate the dry flour into the wet well.

"You were right," Luciana said. "This is chemistry. Cooking is the magic combination of science meets art."

"Perhaps, then, I'll have an aptitude for it, after all."

"I think children should be taught basic cooking. Not only for practical survival purposes, but it's an excellent way to learn mathematics, don't you think?"

"Teaching children is something you've given a lot of thought to."

Luciana's forehead creased. Yes, of course, she'd contemplated how she'd like to teach if she ever had the chance. To make learning engaging and fun, and a discovery.

"Can I ask you something?" Gio reached over with the side of his wrist to brush some flour that had landed on Luciana's nose. "When you marry King Agustin and you develop these resorts on the island that are to bring jobs to your people, won't those employees need child care?"

"Yes, why?"

"Shouldn't that be provided for them, organized to make it a workable lifestyle for families?"

"Yes, of course."

"Why couldn't *you* play a part in that? You've told me that issues regarding children have always been on your official agenda, so it wouldn't be coming out of nowhere."

Luciana kneaded her pasta, unable to look Gio in the eye as she answered, "Neither my father nor my future husband would be in favor of that."

"Doesn't what *you* want matter?"

What she didn't want was to lament about the realities that awaited her when she returned to Izerote. All she wanted was to be here right now, completely in the moment, with this mind-blowing man at her side who encouraged her to spread her wings. To see how high she could fly.

"It's unbearable to me, Luci, to accept the idea of you returning to a life where you are limited."

"I must. And it's as much my fault as anyone else's. I allowed my father to lock me up in the palace tower."

"What do you mean?"

"My mother died when I was eleven. A mentally unstable man crashed his car directly into the one she was riding in, killing her instantly."

"How terrible."

"By the time I was a teenager I could tell that my father was a broken man. So I dedicated myself to him. I decided to never cause him any pain. We're all each other has."

"He wasn't able to get over her death."

"My mother was not a happy woman and kept herself distant. I never really knew her. She and my father didn't have romantic love. But the sense of duty that was instilled in him meant he should have somehow protected her from harm, and he couldn't forgive himself for not being able to."

"So now he goes to every length to shield you?"

"He tries to protect all of Izerote from *everything*, which is why time has stood still for our people. And he keeps me as some sort of symbol of that. And I let him."

"I give you credit. I think if it was me, I would run away never to return."

"It's not all bad. I don't take for granted that I live a life of privilege."

"Do you?"

Those two words dangled in the air.

After crumbly messes of flour mixed with egg had been miraculously converted to smooth balls of shiny dough, they were set aside to rest. The cooking students were invited to have a glass of wine and sample olive oils during the break.

Across the market floor, past the produce vendors with their stacks of ripe fruits and vegetables of every hue, Luciana eyed two men in black suits who seemed to be watching her and Gio. They both wore earpieces. She'd seen a couple of similar-looking men when they were shopping for jeans. Was it paranoia, or was she being followed? It wouldn't surprise her if her father knew her whereabouts. Perhaps he didn't trust her note that promised she'd return to the island in time for her wedding. And who could blame him?

"Gio, inconspicuously turn around. Do you see a couple of men over there looking at us?" She gestured with her head in their direction.

But when they both subtly turned to check, the men were gone.

Chef Katia called them back into the kitchen. She showed them how to roll out the dough with a rolling pin and then feed it through a pasta machine. The process looked easier than it was. Luciana and Gio hand cranked their creations through the rollers. Eventually, they ended up with even sheets of pasta that they proudly showed each other. "You should be able to see the outline of your fingers underneath," Chef Katia instructed.

Luciana tested hers by lifting it up in her hand. Gio leaned over and laced his fingers through hers so that they could see their hands holding each other's through the veil of the thin pasta. They pivoted their hands this way and that, grooving on the sight of their fingers under the dough. At the sight of their hands beautifully intertwined, Luciana bit her lip.

Chef Katia demonstrated how to cut their sheets into thin strips that were ready to be tossed into boiling water. She had pots of water ready for those who wanted to cook and eat their pasta then and there. Some students, like Gio and Luciana, instead put theirs into plastic bags to take with them.

"Let's go home and try again," he said, making Luciana think about something different from dinner.

On the ride back to the villa, Gio put his long arm around her shoulders. She adored the smell of him, always clean and fresh. Her head rested so nicely against his solid and wide chest. When they were together, she was truly *with* him. Maybe that was what it was like to be in love, in harmony both physically and mentally.

Could she stay like this? Or could he come home with her where they'd demand the life they were entitled to? Why couldn't he be by her side at the palace, sharing dreams and passions?

Way down inside, she knew that was more make-believe. What had passed between them last night was only another souvenir for her memory box. The ex-virgin princess had simply got a taste of forbidden fruit, a secret she would carry to her grave. But that was it. It most definitely shouldn't happen again. It couldn't. It was too dangerous. She knew it and sensed that Gio did, too.

So why was it that after they'd successfully cooked and eaten a delicious pasta dinner, Luciana found herself sitting on Gio's lap in the courtyard? Why was she kissing and being kissed with an urgency that nothing in her life had ever demanded before? And why did it feel unquestionably right rather than wrong when, once again, he laid her down on his bed, his potent body hovering over hers as he showed her rhapsodies she had no knowledge existed?

CHAPTER EIGHT

GIO WALKED WITH a spring in his step like a schoolboy as he rushed to meet Luciana after work. He had told her to meet him in front of the Basilica Santa Maria Novella, the Gothic landmark church near the train station. It was hard to believe how much had happened since that fateful day when she'd arrived by train and he interceded to protect her from those thugs who were attempting to steal her jewels. He'd lived a lifetime since then and was astonished as he acknowledged how big a part of his life Luciana had become in such a short time. That wasn't like him. Yet all he wanted to do was both talk to and listen to her, and he'd had more conversation with her in the past few days than he'd probably had in a year.

Which was why he couldn't get to her fast enough. He hadn't told her where he was taking her, wanting to keep it a surprise. As had become their pattern, they'd meet at dusk while visitor attractions were still open for an hour or two longer. Where he was taking her today wasn't a typical tourist stop, but it was somewhere he thought she'd like.

Can't get to her fast enough. What crazy thoughts he was having. This wasn't supposed to be happening to him, caring whether or not he was with any woman, let alone a special one. Emotions were escaping his control. Sucked into an unexplainable whirlpool, his hours and days were delineated by time spent with Luciana and time waiting to return to her side again.

None of this was in character for him. He dealt in logic and probabilities, in calculus and abstracts that allowed him to understand a technological plane that would mystify the majority of people in the world. Feelings knew no logic, no mathematical equation that could be proved without doubt. He was in an uncharted operating system, and did not know his way around.

Which must have been why his heart skipped when he saw Luciana in the church square. She was wearing the *comfy* jeans, as she had come to call them, making him think of a carefree young woman on a metro bus. She looked like a proper Luci, a girl who dressed in whatever whim dictated, whose day was her own. Not one who lived by the regimented precision she had described on Izerote.

Was Luciana talking to someone? Yes, she was conversing with a woman who had a mop of hair pulled up in a bun. A few young children were running around them in a circle. Had she struck up a conversation with a stranger, or had the woman approached her?

One of the children pulled on Luciana's leg and she bent down to talk to the little girl. The expression on Luciana's face was one of pure dedication as she appeared to be answering the child's question. Gio noticed her easy manner with the girl, just as a boy grabbed her hand from the other side. Instead of being flustered Luciana divided her time between the two children, until she and the other woman were laughing by the time Gio approached.

"This is my friend Chiara. I think I told you we had met a few days ago."

"Oh, yes, the teacher. Nice to meet you."

"And you." Chiara called out, "Antonio, stop torturing that pigeon."

The boy ran closer and Luciana said to him, "Sweetheart, when you touch the pigeons you scare them. They don't like to be petted like dogs and cats do."

"Okay." The boy shrugged his shoulders.

"Chiara was taking the kids out for a walk and we ran into each other."

"Luci is actually wonderful with the children. She's been helping me."

"I don't doubt it." Gio glanced to Luciana, who looked like the ultimate Madonna with cherubic children circling her.

"I have to go. Their parents will be picking them up soon. Nice to meet you, Gio."

"You, too."

After watching Chiara and the children scurry away from the square, Gio pecked Luciana's cheek. "How was your time at the Uffizi Gallery?"

"Magnificent, of course. Where are we going tonight?"

Gio led her down a street off the church's piazza. They reached the front of a very unassuming building with big brass doorknobs.

"What is this?"

He turned the knobs and opened the doors. "The Firenze Profumo Farmaceutica. It's one of the oldest pharmacies and cosmetic shops in the world."

They entered the formal salon.

"Oh, my gosh." Her eyes lit up as she took it all in.

They had stepped back in time. Heavy burgundy drapery with gold pull cords lined the walls. Elaborate chandeliers hung from high frescoed ceilings, casting a yellowish light. A few red velvet benches were placed here and there atop the tapestried rug. Behind one long glass counter, three attendants assisted customers.

"The smell is incredible." Luciana inhaled the floral and spicy aromas that permeated the entire space as they walked farther in.

"The Dominican friars established this in the thirteenth century," Gio explained.

Luciana was drawn to the rows of glass cases. They held a dazzling array of perfumes, colognes, creams, lotions, shampoos and soaps. Some were in re-creations of bottles that matched the era when the particular product was created, such as the Acqua di Caterina from the 1500s, commissioned exclusively for Caterina de' Medici of the famous Florentine family. Other products were in simple bottles, pots and jars bearing the label of the *farmaceutica*.

"Come this way."

They passed into an interior parlor.

"What's this?"

The room had a large glass table in the center on which sat dozens of small amber bottles with droppers. One wall was filled with books. “Those were written by the friars, the original recipes for their preparations,” Gio explained. Glass doors opened to an herb garden. “They make balms and ointments and tonic remedies here.”

“How do you know about this place?”

“The de’ Medici family, the leaders of the Florentine Renaissance, were proponents of medicine. In fact, their name is where the word *medicine* is derived from. Florence has always been a place to celebrate the healing powers and versatility of botanicals. My grandmother and hers before her and probably relatives even before that shopped here.”

“How lovely of you to bring me.”

“This is the room where they develop perfumes. I thought you might like to create a fragrance that’s uniquely yours. When you smell it, you can remember your visit to Florence.” *And me*, Gio thought but didn’t say aloud. He hoped she would always remember him, as heaven knew he’d always remember her. More than he thought he should if his prediction proved correct.

Walking the streets of Florence with her

had become natural now. When he wasn't with her, he felt off. Not quite right. Incomplete. Together, they seemed to grab something out of thin air and form it into something real and weighty.

A lone tear escaped from Luciana's eyes.

"Why are you crying?"

"I'm not. I'm just so touched that you thought of this. About making a perfume."

A middle-aged woman with her hair pulled tightly back and wearing a white lab coat entered the salon. "*Buona giornata*, I am Imilia and I will be assisting you today." She pointed to one set of the glass dropper bottles on the table. "These are some of our essential oils. Perhaps you'd like to start with one of those for our top note and then we'll add on to customize a fragrance."

Imilia laid several strips of testing paper on the table. From each bottle she squeezed a drop for them to smell.

After a few, Luciana was clear that she liked orange blossom.

"Now we'll choose a central note and a base note or two."

Gio loved seeing how seriously Luciana took the task, smelling the test strips several times before she eliminated any of them.

Selections were eventually made.

"Perfume is best aged. The scents will meld over time."

Gio whispered into Luciana's ear, "Think of me six months from today when the perfume has mellowed but my memories of you won't have."

As soon as those words fell out of his mouth, Gio regretted saying them. Soon enough Her Royal Highness Princess Luciana de la Isla de Izerote would not only leave Florence, but would leave him. Forever.

There was a king to wed. Heirs to produce. Her fates were decided. It was cruel to encourage her to remember him. Quite the opposite would be kinder. If he really cared about her, he'd hope she'd forget him the minute she left Italian soil.

How could he have allowed them to make love? Two nights in a row, no less. Even though he knew she wanted to as much as he did, he should have resisted. So what that their lips fit so seamlessly to each other's? So what that Luciana's lissome body went boneless against his, meeting his angles with her pliable curves? And so what that now they anticipated each other's movements, each of them in constant undulation around each other as if they were no longer independent beings?

She was never to be his.

No matter what, they couldn't make love again. What happened couldn't be undone, but Gio could keep from making matters worse. It was the least he could do. Monarchy aside, Luciana was an inexperienced young woman. He should have been the stronger one. Defended her. The last thing he'd want to do was hurt her.

Nothing everlasting could ever be between them.

Could it?

Imilia asked if Luciana would like to name her fragrance and have a personalized label for the bottle.

"Let's call it Luci," she answered without hesitation. Of course. Luci being a different person from Luciana. The bottle of Luci that she'd no doubt keep hidden would bear witness to secrets the princess might never tell another living soul.

From the bottle that would bear her name, she rubbed a few drops of her fragrance onto the inside of her wrist, which she brought to her nose. Then she presented it to Gio to reconfirm that the scent was appealing. He lifted her delicate wrist, his fingertips memorizing every one of the tiny bones under her porcelain skin. The blend of the orange blossom, cloves, cinnamon and bergamot was a heady and pleasing combination.

Before he could stop himself, he topped off the examination of the inside of her wrist with a kiss. Just what he'd meant *not* to do. And without realizing ahead of time that the barest amount of physical contact would reverberate through his body and make him want to do things to Princess Luciana right then and there that would have the Dominican friars rolling in their graves.

"Chiara!" Luciana waved when, out for another walk in the Santa Maria Novella piazza, she spotted her new friend and the kids.

"Luci. Come sit. The children are playing." Chiara pointed to a bench that allowed her to keep a close watch on her charges.

"So is that handsome Gio your lover?"

"No. He's just a friend." Luciana didn't know how to answer. Yes, she had made love with him. No, he was not her lover in any true sense of the word. Yes, she wished more than anything in the world that he was.

The princess would return to Izerote changed in more ways than would be visible to the eye. Hair cut and dyed, she'd have to face her father's scrutiny over something as petty as her appearance. He'd never know that she'd been forever altered internally, as well. That she'd known the earthquake of a man and a woman in the throes of passion, the planet moving beneath them, modifying the universe so that it could never go back to exactly how it was before. More important, not her father nor her future husband nor any other living soul would know that she herself had shifted like the tectonic plates under the earth, and would never be the same again.

"I saw how your eyes shined when he met you here yesterday," Chiara continued. "And he had the face of a man who thought he was the luckiest one alive when he found you in the crowd. Smells like lovers to me," she said in a cute lilt that made Luciana laugh.

"It's complicated."

"Isn't it always?"

Two of the boys were having a duel with the plastic spoons that they had been using to eat a snack. Jamming their implements at each other in a way that was going to lead to someone getting hurt. Chiara called out, "Boys, it is a gentleman's duel. Take two steps backward and bow to each other."

Which they did, eking a smile out of the two women.

"Do you have a boyfriend?"

"I go out with a nice enough guy, but he's

not *the one*. My eyes don't flicker when I'm with him like yours did with Gio. I'm leaving Firenze soon, so it's best not to get serious."

The words banged between Luciana's ears. Of course when someone was planning to leave the place where they were, it was best not to allow any meaningful relationships to develop. That was so obvious Luciana would bet that even these children having spoon duels would understand. Any idiot would.

Except her, apparently. She did know that her feelings toward Gio had passed serious days ago and now had moved into critical. Which was not good.

"When are you going?" Luciana tried to distract herself by asking about Chiara's impending move.

"I'm half there now and half here on the days I work. I commute by train." Chiara had told her that her family, her mother and two sisters who were also teachers, were opening up a school in Salerno. A town in the south near Naples, it was a four-hour train ride from Florence. "To open a school is not a way to make a lot of money, but it's what we love. So I go down as often as I can to paint walls and buy furniture and network with the people who live there."

"Do you have commitments from families

that are going to send their children to the school?"

"Oh, yes. We already have forty students enrolled."

"That's amazing!"

Luciana admired Chiara. Not only had she pursued her goal of becoming a teacher, but now she was opening her own business at it.

"What about you?"

To the outside world, they must look like two friends sharing a chat during lunch while the children in their care play. Perhaps that outside world might see Luciana as a teacher, too. Passersby would think them two young gals who were dishing about boyfriends and aspirations. "If Gio isn't your lover, what are you doing with him?"

Waltzing through the cloudy haze of a beautiful dream she never wanted to wake up from?

"I'm only in Florence for a short time," Luciana uttered softly. "I'm leaving, too."

"Ah, Gio was your passionate Italian fling?"

Princess Luciana winced at that characterization, thinking it cheapened the situation. Although perhaps that's exactly how she would recollect it decades from now.

"You're sad to leave him."

Chiara had no idea how right she was. But

Her Royal Highness would have so much to distract her when she returned to the palace. There would be dull diplomatic lunches to attend, boring dedications to make appearances at and a man she barely knew to marry. How would she find the time in her schedule to pine for the magical man in Florence?

"I am."

"Have you rubbed the snout of Il Porcellino?"

"Not yet." Luciana knew about the legend of the bronze figure near the Mercato Nuovo. Lore had it that if you rubbed the nose of the boar, it meant you would return to Florence.

Luciana would do that before her trip was over, although her wish would be bittersweet.

Because even if she was to return, it would be too late for her and Gio.

"You don't want to go home, Luci?"

"I don't, and yet I can't stay here."

"Do you want to come work for me in Salerno?"

"Do I what?" Luciana could hardly believe the words she was hearing.

"Work for me. I can't hire you as a teacher until you earn a degree in early childhood education. But you can assist us. The children clearly love you."

Laugh or cry. Both options were equally viable. Princess Luciana de la Isla de Izerote had been offered her first job. In her chosen profession. In some families, that would be cause for celebration. In hers, it was a disgrace. *Laugh or cry.*

Even though she was supposed to have another two weeks in Florence, her departure was imminent.

The proverbial clock ticked.

Walls closed in.

There'd be no escape.

"A job."

With every blink of her eyes, she saw flashes of red.

Warning lights.

Danger signals.

Because Princess Luciana could not ignore that, once again, across the piazza, she noticed two men in black suits staring directly at her as they spoke into earpieces. Her stomach sank to her knees as the reality became impossible to dispute.

Chiara handed her a business card, which Luciana numbly slid into her jeans pocket alongside the pocket money Gio had insisted she carry.

"You can think about it. Let me know in the next few days."

* * *

Was she really thinking what she was thinking? The events of this past week made Luciana doubt every stronghold she'd ever embraced. Heady concepts like responsibility and sacrifice, honor and privilege, obligation and liberty were now all under question. Anything and everything was up for grabs.

Would she really be able to pull off the idea that was fighting for a place in her rational mind? It made sense and it made no sense at the same time. When Viggo dropped her off at her requested location, Luciana had been so lost in her dilemma that she'd hardly noticed the drive. She asked him to wait and stepped out of the car.

The Piazzale Michelangelo was a public square on a hill that afforded a breathtaking view of the city. From the river and its bridges to the bell tower of the Badia Fiorentina to the Duomo to the Tuscan mountains beyond, its breadth was spectacular. Overwhelming to take in all at once, the panorama had been known to make people weep. No different for the princess. Tears rolled down her face in a steady stream, chilled by the hilltop breeze.

The first tears were for Gio, whom in any scenario, she'd be torn from like a bandage that rips away the skin underneath it when it is removed. Other tears represented trepidation about what she was planning. If she failed, she'd have made even a bigger mess than what she'd already created. If she succeeded, there would be no turning back.

There were tears for the mother she barely knew. Who was unable to rise to her own duty. Although she didn't cause her own death, her spirit was laid to rest before her marriage at age eighteen. Part of Luciana's decision would be in her mother's honor.

Still different tears were for her father, whom in spite of all of this, she loved dearly and risked wounding. A young man himself when her mother died, he was ill-equipped to parent an eleven-year-old girl and turned to fear of loss as his only guidance.

And, because it had transformed her so drastically that no matter what road she took it could never be one she'd already traveled, she cried for Florence, which she'd miss every day of her life.

Luciana got back in the car and had Viggo drop her off at her next destination.

Chiara had been right. Il Porcellino was quite the tourist attraction. The open-air Mercato Nuovo was in full swing near the bronze boar, and the whole area was alive with Florentine bustle. As she'd seen elsewhere in the city, budding artists used colored chalk to draw replicas of famous paintings onto the pavement of city streets, putting out tip cups for passersby to show their appreciation. Many of the chalk renderings were excellent. Luciana took note of the young artists and wondered what their lives must be like, living and practicing their craft in this inspiring place.

Visitors queued up to touch the famous boar, and the princess took her place behind a tour group, all of whom wore matching plastic nameplates around their necks. English, German and Japanese were just three of the languages she heard around her. The bronze *porcellino*, or piglet, was covered in a green-brown patina except for its snout, which had been polished to a sheen by all the attention bestowed on it.

While she waited, she pivoted her head as far as she could to the left and then all the way to the right to take in the scene at the Mercato Nuovo until she found what she knew she would. Past a vendor specializing in wallets and belts, two men in black suits watched her. She couldn't tell if they were the same men from the piazza with Chiara earlier today, but it didn't matter.

She'd seen men in black suits outside the

clothing store when she and Gio were shopping for jeans. There were two at the Mercato Centrale when she and Gio took the pasta-making class. Then today at the piazza. Part of her had been trying to deny the reality of what they represented. Now as her breath tightened and a blush burned her cheeks, she could pretend no longer.

King Mario de la Isla de Izerote had found her. Maybe he'd had her followed all along. She no longer believed that she was going to get the full three weeks of escape she had planned before returning to Izerote and her wedding. Today was her seventh day. A hunch in her gut told her it was her last.

This schedule was probably designed by her father. He, no doubt, instructed his security detail to have her located and surveilled but if she seemed safe, to let her have her silly little fun. Rage inched up her throat as she fully comprehended what must have happened. That she hadn't even had the small measure of freedom she'd hoped to cherish for the rest of her life. All she'd been granted was a longer chain than usual.

When it was her turn to touch the bronze boar's nose, she stroked it as lovingly as she would have had it been Gio's face. She threw her arms around its neck and held herself close. Because she was in love. With Luci, the young teacher who had the most marvelous boyfriend in the world.

If rubbing Il Porcellino's snout meant she would return, she'd rub it a hundred times before she let go.

Thank you, Florence.

Thank you, Gio.

Finally, she backed away to let the people who were waiting have their turn.

As she did, poison blackened her insides when she heard an unfamiliar male voice behind her say, "Princess Luciana, may we speak with you for a moment?"

Luciana didn't turn around to acknowledge him.

"And we'd like to speak with the gentleman you've been keeping company with."

Those words sliced like a lash across her back. The most unbearable consequence of her actions would be if Gio was brought into the chaos she'd made. He had plenty of his own issues to deal with. He'd been nothing but kind to her and deserved better.

Blood vessels throbbed through Luciana's skull. What she was scheming was her only hope. A far-fetched Hail Mary. Worth a try because, at this point, she had nothing to lose.

She suddenly bulleted forward and dashed into the outdoor marketplace.

If she could just get away from these security men right now, she'd carry out her plan immediately. Making an abrupt right turn, she tore through an aisle of merchants who were all selling tablecloths and bed linens displayed on hooks so that the fabrics danced in the afternoon wind. As the bedsheets swayed, Luciana was able to maneuver quickly between one and around another until she got to the other end of the market.

A quick glance backward confirmed that she'd done it. The men weren't trailing her!

With no time to wait for Viggo, whom she'd asked to return in an hour, she hailed a taxi to return her to the villa. Which she slipped into, seemingly unnoticed. As she bounded up the stairs of her guest cottage, her heart thundered. The ticking bomb was about to explode. Time to hurry.

She picked up the phone on the night table beside her bed. It had been seven days since she'd held a phone, the hard plastic harsh and now unfamiliar in her hand as she punched in a number. "Chiara, it's Luci."

After the call, she yanked her suitcase out of the closet and tossed it on the bed, unzipping it to unpack the items she had left buried inside. The ones she had hoped never to need. The ones that were now her last chance.

"Luciana?" Gio's voice called up to her bedroom from the courtyard a half hour later. "Luciana?"

What was he doing home? It was hours before he was to finish work and join her for their usual early-evening sightseeing. They were to finally tour the Duomo, which she had been greatly looking forward to.

"I'm up here," she yelled through the open doors to the Juliet balcony, hoping not to have to see him.

"I was so worried," he continued shouting up. "Viggo said he went to pick you up but you weren't there."

"I'm fine, Gio. Go back to the office."

Luciana had already written him a note to leave on the table in the courtyard. An in-person goodbye was more than she could handle.

"Come to the balcony, Luciana."

"No, Gio. Please go back to work." It was agony to tell him to go, but if he knew what she was planning, he'd try to stop her.

"Luciana! Luciana!"

The low timbre of his bellow was too much for her to fight. She'd allow herself one last time the sight of his exquisite face and the tall muscular body that had educated her in ecstasies she'd never expected to learn.

With a last check in the mirror before she'd have to tell Gio the truth, Princess Luciana confirmed that her look was complete. When she'd arrived in Barcelona after stowing away on that supply ship leaving Izerote, she'd bought not one but two disguises. Her *just in case* would be put to the test right now.

The boy's brown suit fit her about right, appropriately shapeless to skim over any womanly curves. The white shirt and brown shoes matched it. And the dark wig cut above the ears gave her the appearance of a teenaged boy, perhaps on his way to a school interview or reluctantly forced to get dressed up for an occasion. No, the delicate skin and regal bones of her face were not very masculine, but she knew that some boys had fine features. Walking down the street, no one would give her a second glance.

She stepped out onto the Juliet balcony to face Gio.

"The men who have been following you?" Gio asked upon seeing her in the ensemble.

"How did you know?"

"I saw them, too. I didn't say anything because I hoped you hadn't noticed. I didn't want to ruin your precious time here with the news."

"I can't go back to Izerote, Gio. Not after everything that happened here. Not after you."

She inhaled the full view the balcony afforded. The old buildings, the chirps of birds sharing a song with the horns of taxicabs. The splendid mixture of the ancient and the modern that was this city. And the high-tech billionaire here who'd keep her heart.

Luciana moved away from the balcony and back into her bedroom. Closing her suitcase, with the bag of jewels that were her only currency inside, she made her way down the stairs and out to the courtyard where Gio stood waiting.

"Where are you going?"

"Chiara offered me a job at her new school in the south, near Naples. If I can get away without being caught, maybe I have a chance. I'll disappear there. I'll find a way to contact my father and tell him that I'm not coming home."

Desperation had driven her to the unconceivable.

"Don't leave," Gio implored. "We'll figure it out. There has to be a way."

"There is none. Not when they're closing in

on me. On us. As it is, I've dragged you into this further than I ever meant to."

His hands circled her wrists, handcuffing her in his grasp. "No. You're not leaving."

"Maybe someday I'll be able to return. I rubbed the nose of the boar. Maybe a Florence miracle will be ours."

"I'll help you. I'll drive you there. At least then I'll know exactly where you are. When it's safe we'll be together again."

"No. They'll follow you. Go back to the office. When they question you, say I disappeared without a trace. Say you don't know anything."

"You've never been on your own. I'll worry about you every day of my life. I can't let you go."

"Let me go, Gio. For both of our sake. You have your company to protect. And I can't have you take the place of my father. I have to try something of my own or else I'll never know what freedom is."

She lifted up on her tiptoes and craned her neck so that her lips would reach his. For one goodbye kiss that contained the sun, the moon and all the stars in the sky.

Then she broke away from him, grabbed her suitcase and fled out through the entrance tunnel that led to the street.

Chiara was to meet her at the train station, so Luciana rushed in that direction, disguise in place. But within seconds, a black car screeched to a stop beside her on the street. The two men who had been following her at the bronze boar got out of the car.

"Princess Luciana, at your father's request we are here to take you home."

Speechless and unsure what to do, she covered her mouth with her hand. In her heart of hearts, she knew she'd never be able to outrun these men, and even if she did they—or others like them—would be back again the next day. It was a foolish attempt. Her father had decided that it was time for her journey to come to an end. Just as she always figured he would.

She looked back toward the villa. Gio had chased after her and stood a few paces behind. The two men glared at him, and then one of them took hold of Princess Luciana's arm. The other opened the passenger door of the black car. He stated flatly, "Time to go."

Using no small amount of force, the man began to marshal Princess Luciana into the car. In doing so, her wig came off in his hand. The blond lob that had now become her real hairstyle spilled around her face as tears pooled in her eyes. She turned back one last time and called out, "I love you, Gio! I love you."

With that, she surrendered into the back seat and the door was closed after her. The two men got into the front seat, and from the clicks and beeps she heard, she knew she had been securely locked into her motorized jail.

Her Royal Highness Princess Luciana de la Isla de Izerote jerked around to look out the back window as the car pulled away. Gio ran toward her, sprinting after the car, picking up his own speed as the vehicle did, too. But when the car took a big lead over him, the last thing she saw was his mouth saying something to her. She'd spend the rest of her life wondering what it was.

CHAPTER NINE

"I LOVE YOU, too, Luciana! I love you, too."

Gio stared blankly out of his office window replaying the words he had screamed at the top of lungs yesterday as the black car drove his heart away from his body.

Yesterday. When the world was a different place. Because Luci was in it. Luci, the whip-smart, fun-loving, sensual breath of fresh air that had shaken Gio to his core, was gone forever. Oh, certainly Princess Luciana de la Isla de Izerote still lived and breathed. To marry and bear children, and hopefully remain healthy and strong for decades to come. But the part of her that had spent this enchanting week with Gio had disappeared into thin air as quickly as she had arrived.

What was she doing right now? Begging her father's and her fiancé's forgiveness? For stealing seven days? Who could blame her for wanting that? How could that be considered an offense? Gio's fists clenched at the injustice.

For her.

For him.

She was supposed to have three weeks. He'd been planning to take her to his family's vineyard in Chianti. To show her the charming coastal towns of the Cinque Terra. The lush terrain of the Emilio Romagna region. Perhaps a few days in Venice.

Cruelly, their time together was cut short. But the week they'd had changed the course of his life. Because once you loved, you could no longer pretend that it wasn't important. That it was something you could live without. That it wasn't worth the risk.

That it wouldn't destroy a person once it was gone.

Destruction wasn't an option for Gio. Family loyalty demanded that he run this empire. The responsibility was on him.

He turned his concentration to work. As he drafted a public statement to announce the next generation of DDR SDRAM that would render everything currently on the market obsolete, Princess Luciana's suggestions to him came to mind. She'd remind him that it wasn't technical mumbo jumbo that the public would respond to. It was people being their genuine selves that made an impression.

How right she was. His fingers flew over the keys as he typed. Grasstech might be a leader in the computer industry, but it was a company started by one man and now under the care of his sons. With thousands of employees throughout the world, each of whose diligent work contributed to the company's success. For the new RAM, Park Baek Yeol in Seoul had worked for years on its development. Adil Pannu's group in Mumbai tested hundreds of designs until they found one that could be produced at much less expense than its predecessor.

Once Gio had crafted a statement he was pleased with, he was ready to share it with his marketing team. After hitting the send button, he shut down his computer for the night.

As he was leaving the office, Samuele locked in step with him in the corridor. "*Mio amico*, we must decide where we are going to manufacture the biometric products. This is an enormous undertaking for us. Have you given it any thought?"

"I will, Samuele. Thank you. I want you to know how much I appreciate you."

"Why are you so wistful?"

Gio couldn't bring himself to explain about Luciana. Not yet, anyway.

At home, he pushed open the door to the villa. There was no doubt that the envelope on the table in the courtyard was for him. Luciana had left it, hoping to make a clean exit without having to say goodbye. Luck, or serendipity, spoiled her plot. As bad as it was to watch her being driven away by her keepers, it would have been far worse not to have bid her farewell. After she'd been transported long out of sight, he'd shuffled back to the villa but couldn't bear to read her note.

Recognizing the Grasstech logo embossed on the top left corner of the envelope, Gio nodded to himself. Of course, even in order to leave him a message, she'd had to borrow an envelope and probably the piece of paper it was written on. Which of his pens had she used? Anything he had was hers for the asking, yet it brought a crinkle to his face that she hadn't brought royal stationery with her from Izerote. No, she was too busy bringing wigs and palace jewels in her attempt to clinch time without her tiara for just one holiday.

Gio slid his finger under the flap to open the envelope. Having never seen her handwriting, he was awed by its feminine and stately precision. Every line symmetrical, every word incorporating as many swirly flourishes as it could hold.

Ache pushed through him as he appreciated the beauty in the way Luciana had written his name.

Gio.

You have no idea how much you have given me in addition to your generosity. You have shown me a modern world full of excitement and potential, where ambition and innovation are celebrated.

I vow to you now that I will find a way to teach that to my children, and to tell them about the brilliant man in Florence who taught it to me.

You are the only man I will ever love, and I will love you until my dying day.

Yours forever, Luci.

Uncharacteristic mist filled Gio's eyes as he peered up to the Juliet balcony of Luciana's guest cottage, knowing only too painfully that she wouldn't be appearing. Because darn if the words he yelled as he tried in vain to catch up to that car weren't true. He loved her. And now that he knew what love was, he was sure it was something he'd never known before.

With Francesca, until she betrayed him, there was lust. And the commonality of working in the same industry. A similar lifestyle. Work came first, and there was never any worry about dividing his energies.

But his heart never lurched out of his chest at the mere thought of Francesca. He'd surely never had sunny visions of a home built together and children to share it with. A foundation that sparked his creativity. Celebrating successes and enduring challenges as one, an entity stronger than the sum of its parts.

Luciana made those possibilities dance through his head. In fact, he couldn't stop obsessing over them. So much so that those visions had bent to include royal life. It would take adjustment, but he could see himself accepting the obligations and rules that would come with being at the princess's side. They'd find a way to protect some amount of a private life for themselves. Love gave everything potential.

After sitting down at the courtyard table to pick at the pasta left over from their cooking class, Gio let his mind travel to faraway places. To the island of Izerote. To imagine what his heart was doing at this very moment. To miss her.

When he had wallowed for as long as he

could stand, he forced his mind to turn a corner. The next issue on his agenda was where the biometric products were to be produced. He could give them to one of the India plants, although the crews there already had plenty to do. In fact, he'd like to shift some of the ongoing manufacturing he had operating out of Mumbai to somewhere else. The Tokyo plants were overworked, too. A new location might be what was in order. The components were all small parts that didn't require massive production equipment, so that opened up a lot of options.

The strangest germ of an idea popped into his mind. With some research and phone calls, he began to envision a prospect. The next morning, he summoned Samuele to his office and included his father at the winery in the discussion via FaceTime. Gio announced where he was taking new manufacturing.

If he had his way.

Which he was about to find out.

"Samuele, I have no idea how to reach my destination. Book a trip for me."

"Your Royal Highness, may I ask you to lift up your arms?" Three dress fitters swarmed around Luciana. She obliged, although the tight lace sleeves of the wedding gown didn't allow much flexibility of movement. "Just a bit higher, Princess, please. Most appreciated."

With the three-paneled mirror set up in front of a dais that provided easy access for alterations to the gown, Luciana was on display like a pirouetting ballerina in a child's wind-up jewelry box. One tailor slowly circled the bottom of the gown, pinning it for a perfect hemline. The other two attended to the rest of the fit.

"Would you prefer us to add a large lace flower at the waistline?" one of them asked. The question caught Luciana by surprised as it was the first one anyone had asked her since she was returned to the palace yesterday. Every last detail of her upcoming wedding had been decided on by the royal wedding planners and her father. She supposed that having disappeared for seven days she had further forfeited her right to any say in the matter. Although she was the bride, she felt like a mannequin that was only one element in the whole of the affair, of equal importance to the cake or the table settings. The fitter held a lace rose to the waistband of the gown. Then withdrew it for comparison.

The dress was so undeniably hideous the princess didn't think it much mattered whether yet one more adornment was added. At her father's request, the design had been modeled on the one worn by her great-great-grandmother at her own wedding. While a style that was hopelessly out of date could have a kind of retro charm, this one did not. She was reminded that the unbearable confines of this gown were what propelled her to finally stow away on that supply boat, and to take her fateful trip to Italy.

A stiff collar led to a fitted lace bodice and sleeves. The silk layer under the lace extended upward almost to the neckline, eliminating any hint of sexiness or even femininity to the décolleté area. Past the waistband, the skirt portion was full-on poof, round with gigantic petticoats that made her think she might be wearing a hot air balloon. Perhaps she could float up toward the clouds and be carried away.

A veil was affixed to her head. It was long enough to hoist beachcombers from Barcelona onto Izerote. The ensemble was finished off with uncomfortable matching pumps with decorative buckles—yes, buckles—encrusted with crystals.

"Princess?" The fitter was still waiting on her opinion about the lace rose at the waistband.

Luciana lazily shrugged her shoulders. She was defeated. Gio was right. She'd never been independent and she never would be. Why should she decide if the gown should have a flower on it? Let the dresser choose.

The royal planners had buzzed themselves into a tizzy as soon as the princess had been delivered back to the palace, with everyone told that she had been temporarily called off the island to lend her support to an urgent humanitarian crisis. A palace public relations spin, in action. But which, in essence, was accurate as far as she was concerned. Although, even if they knew the truth, she wouldn't have expected any sympathy from anyone at the palace about her own human need to soul search before she dedicated the rest of her life to the service of the crown.

Returning wasn't so easy, as she'd been changed by her journey. So her new goal would be to become more like her mother. To shut down, check out, not have an opinion about anything. She'd keep the life she wished she led alive in her mind, but walk through her real one.

"Kindly allow me a few minutes of privacy with my daughter." King Mario de la Isla de Izerote's stomp, then voice, reverberated off the walls as he shooed away the wedding staff.

They assisted the princess down from the alterations dais before taking their leave.

Surely Luciana's father was the person least able to understand why she had to go to Florence. In fact, he hadn't even welcomed her back last night, merely sending a representative to convey his relief at her safe return. His wrath was to be one of the prices she'd pay for her defiance.

It was worth it, though, she confirmed to herself with a bite of her lower lip. "Father," she exhaled bravely.

"What have you done to your hair?"

"I had it cut and colored."

"That much is obvious."

As was expected of her, Luciana had always shown her father the utmost respect and deference. She loved him. If only he'd been a perceptive enough parent to see that spending her life isolated on this island where time stood still was a fate his daughter couldn't bear.

"I didn't mean to cause you worry," she stated with her head slightly bowed so she wouldn't have to make eye contact. "That's why I left you a note promising my return."

"It would have been proper protocol to ask my permission, not to stow away on a supply boat."

As she suspected, she'd been surveilled from the very beginning of her voyage.

"If you were following my every move, Father, why didn't you allow me the three weeks my note to you promised?"

"I received information that you were keeping company with a man. There was an incident involving *gelato*," he spat, as if it were a bitter taste in his mouth, "that my operatives interpreted as highly improper. I decided it best to sever that liaison as soon as possible, in your own best interest."

The princess brought her hand over her mouth in absolute mortification.

After a painful silence she said, "My best interest. I've tried to be a perfect daughter and a perfect princess."

"Is your idea of a perfect princess who is soon to be married one who cavorts around Florence with a man who isn't her fiancé?"

"That wasn't something I had planned." Nor was falling in love.

"Perhaps. But it was most undignified. We all have rules we must abide by, girl."

"I'm not a girl."

"You have acted like one."

No, he was wrong. For the first time in her life, Luciana had been a steel-eyed, rock-solid adult. Gio had taught her that. In seven short days, she'd learned more about being an adult from him than she had in her entire life.

Amazing Gio. Who thought for himself. From big-picture revelations to infinitesimal technological solutions. How often during her too-brief time with him had he asked her what she wanted and, if she didn't know, challenged her to find her answer? He shaped her into the woman she would now be. Which ruined her at the same time. As it was the man before her now to whom she was truly bound.

"It doesn't matter anymore. We live like museum pieces. We're fossils. I'll just turn to stone like mother did."

"Don't you think I know what you're feeling? I'm not so old that I don't remember what it was to be young. To crave drama and abandon. But I came to accept, as my forefathers did and as you will, too, that the honor and onus of the crown is far more important than any selfish goals that might try to lure us away."

Deep down, Luciana knew that her father was not the enemy. She could blame her fates if she wanted to. What good would that do her in the end?

"You will marry. And bear children. Your days will be full. These longings you have will pass. In time, you'll forget them."

"I don't love King Agustin." She loved Giovanni Grassi. And although she would never see him again, she would hold her love for him like a precious jewel in her hand until her last breath.

"And your mother did not love me." King Mario spoke a truth they both already knew. "Duty, Luciana. You'll truly be an adult when you stop battling your destiny."

Luciana shifted her eyes to the three panels of the dressing mirrors. There she stood in the ugly wedding gown she was to wear when her father would escort her down the aisle. Her father, who'd endured a loveless marriage that produced only one, ungrateful heir. A man who had to receive the middle-of-the-night phone call that his wife had been crushed to death in a car accident. Who did what he thought was his best with his only child.

"King Agustin will bring the jobs to our island we so desperately need," he reminded.

"Eroding our natural resources with tourist resorts? Is that really what's good for our subjects in the long run?"

"Without industry, we have no means to employ our people. It might not be the most inventive idea. However, it's what we're being offered."

Luciana studied her father's reflection in

the three mirrors. His hair was still more pepper than salt. Shoulders that had always stood straight outlined a king with many decades left on the throne.

"Father, we have to think bigger."

"There is no other way."

There simply had to be. Despite her outward resignation, a whisper inside her heart told her she would not walk down that aisle to marry the widower king.

That evening after she'd changed into her nightgown and slippers, Luciana unpacked the suitcase she'd brought to Florence, refusing to let an assistant do it for her. As if they were as fragile as eggshells, she placed the two pairs of boyfriend jeans, the emerald green scarf from the San Lorenzo market and the bottle of Luci perfume in the back of the bottom drawer of her bureau. On top of them, she stacked a pillow and a blanket in the hope that her treasures wouldn't be discovered.

Slipping on her dressing gown, she stepped out onto the terrace of her sitting room. From this vantage point she could survey the north side of the island, facing toward the Spanish mainland.

It was a quiet night on the island, as always, with the crash of the waves against the rock bluffs the only sound to be heard. The sea was rough, water bursting over and over again upon itself with turbulence similar to what she felt in her own center.

No matter how hard she tried, Luciana could not get her mind off Gio. It would eternally haunt her to ponder what it was that he had mouthed to her as the security detail forced her into that black car and squired her away from him. She knew what she hoped he had said. The same words she had screamed out to him, the last words she would ever speak to him.

What was he doing at this very moment? She allowed herself to imagine that it wasn't a palace terrace she looked out from tonight but, instead, the wrought iron Juliet balcony overlooking the courtyard of his villa. With its fragrant lavender and colorful flowers. That he was standing in the midst of it, gazing up at her, his sparkling eyes bright in the dark of night. Beckoning her to come down to him. To his embrace, to his kiss.

The moon tonight was high above the sea. Its distance made her think of a movie plot she'd heard of in which a woman had to be separated from her child. To ease her young son's mind, she promised him that every evening they would each look up to see the same moon. That no matter their distance, because they could both see the moon that would mean they were together.

Oh, Gio, please be looking at the moon. Please be with me tonight.

After staring at the sky with Gio in her heart for as long as she could take it, her eyes drifted to the hills and valleys of the island. To the west sat two abandoned factories, side by side. The eyesores were a constant reminder of the failures of Izerote, one of the reasons why the island's leadership could not provide enough employment for its citizens.

Those two factories had been built by a manufacturing company with the utmost in environmental protections as to not disturb the pristine ecosystems of the island. Engineering and construction were costly in such a remote location. Materials were brought by boat and with the use of the small airstrip that allowed private planes to fly in.

What the business investors had failed to take into consideration was that the machine tools they were manufacturing were heavy in weight and that shipping the finished product back to Barcelona for distribution was so costly all of the profits were eaten up. Within two years, the factories closed and the employees were again out of work. It was not only a catastrophe for the local economy, it was an embarrassment to the king and his advisory team.

If only those factories could be repurposed. If only a small, lightweight product could be manufactured or assembled there, an enterprise that would learn from the mistakes made in the past.

An idea stirred within Luciana.

It might not work. She might not get the necessary parties to agree. Without much knowledge on what the operation would involve, it might be an impossibility.

But what if the impossible was possible? What if?

Her mind swirled with a million thoughts and as many questions. She'd get them all answered. Tomorrow.

By the time dawn broke, she'd spent all night typing everything she'd thought of into her laptop. Ready to take action. She stepped again out onto the terrace to greet the day, assuming that if Gio had seen the same moon, her love would share the sun with her, as well.

Good morning, my exquisite Gio. Can you help me again?

Wasn't it rather early in the morning for a small airplane to be landing onto the island's airstrip?

* * *

As the private plane he'd hired descended for landing, Gio got his first glimpse of the island of Izerote. Luciana had not exaggerated when she'd explained to him just how remote her home was. After the flight to Barcelona, Gio transferred to the small aircraft that shuttled him the rest of the way. Finishing the glass of blood orange juice the lone flight attendant had presented to him earlier, he surveyed the island from the window beside his seat.

Untouched mountain ranges covered much of the terrain. From his vantage point, he spotted three small coastal towns and two more inland. They appeared to be like most towns in Europe. Gio could make out a center area in each, the commercial core dense with buildings erected closely together. Surrounding those in something of a ring were the residential areas with the structures a bit farther apart, homes with small yards. And farther out still from the town center were the more rural properties, some with plots of farmland.

He even saw livestock dotting the green fields. Although not much, according to Luciana, who had explained that most of the food for the island's inhabitants was shipped or flown in. Which explained why goods and services were very expensive, thereby contributing to the reasons many of the citizens were moving off the island. A complex set of issues faced this tiny land. He hoped to be part of the solution.

In a valley, he saw two large buildings that looked like factories. From what Gio could see, they appeared to be empty. If that was the case, his purpose here could be even more easily accomplished. He vaguely remembered Luciana telling him about some ill-thought-out industry that had gone into business here only to fail. That disaster pushed her father even further toward deciding on the arranged marriage between Luciana and the widower king from the neighboring island.

Which was about to be called off, if he had any say about it.

When the palace finally came into view, Gio's pulse quickened. Somewhere within those walls was his love. Picturing Luciana still asleep in a royal bed, no doubt blanketed in the finest of fabrics with her lovely head upon the fluffiest of pillows, filled him with happiness. He could hardly wait to bring his lips to hers. To taste her sweetness. To hold her softness against him.

There were many obstacles to cross before he'd have her in his arms again. But he'd get there.

After touchdown onto the island, Gio located the hired car that had been reserved to take him to the palace. Thank heavens for Samuele at the office in Florence, whom Gio could always count on to get the job done. Samuele had also spoken with palace staff to make an appointment for Gio to speak with King Mario, as a formal meeting with the monarch seemed the most appropriate method of introduction.

Once at the palace entrance, the driver opened the car door for Gio to step out. He took in what he could see of the palace grounds. The whole of it was rather small, befitting the size of the island. Nonetheless it had the foreboding of a fortress with its surrounding barricades of stone.

Upon giving his name at the security gate, Gio was directed to the offices of the king. He passed through entrance doors into a reception foyer. A large oak desk stood in the center. A telephone bank and computer suggested that the desk was useful to operations, although its chair was empty at the moment. Gio took stock of the computer equipment setup and deduced that Wi-Fi was available. Which answered one of the questions he had regarding the idea he'd come to speak to the king about.

A wooden door to Gio's right opened, and a young man in a jacket bearing the palace insignia on the breast pocket emerged but was called back before he exited. He didn't see Gio, and spoke loudly enough to whoever was behind the door that Gio was able to hear them.

"I'll take care of it, King Mario," the attendant continued while Gio eavesdropped. "Also Your Highness, Mr. Giovanni Grassi should be arriving shortly for your appointment. Palace Intelligence has just informed me that Mr. Grassi is the gentleman Princess Luciana had kept company with during her sojourn in Italy."

Uh-oh. Gio had hoped that the king wasn't going to find out the connection between him and Luciana prior to their meeting. He was sure that, as an overprotective father, he would disapprove of Gio after finding out he had been touring Florence with his daughter. Gio wanted to first discuss his plan with the king before he got on to personal business. And, indeed, there were urgent personal matters to discuss. But if the king knew who Gio was at the outset, his anger might bias his ability to hear him out.

"Very well, Your Highness, when Mr. Grassi arrives I'll let him know that you were unexpectedly called away and that your schedule is full for the foreseeable future."

Gio needed to think fast.

If this attendant saw him in the foyer and Gio introduced himself, he'd be escorted out of the palace grounds immediately. Now that the king had gotten word of Gio's association with Luciana, the original course of action was ruled out. He had to find a safe place to reevaluate.

"Thank you, King Mario." The attendant uttered his last words before he closed the door on the king's office.

Not knowing what else to do but disappear before he got caught, Gio hurried down a corridor that led away from the foyer. In his dark blue suit and carrying his Italian leather attaché case, he looked like a legitimate palace visitor. If he encountered anyone along his way, he could feign being lost on his way to an official conference.

Mentally taking note that the corridor was leading him west and then north, he decided that what he needed to do was find Luciana. She'd shelter him and then they'd speak with the king together. Not to mention the fact that every second he'd been apart from her since she left Florence two days ago had been torture. By her side was where he wanted to be as soon as possible, for now and for always.

When he observed a housekeeper wheeling a cart of bed linens up ahead, he assumed he had reached the residential section of the palace. He was on the right track. Trying first one then another, he finally found an unlocked door and ducked into a room before the housekeeper saw him. From behind the closed door he listened until the cart was rolled past.

Tapestries depicting nature scenes adorned the walls of the room he found himself in. Antique or antique-style furniture sat in the center of the room, which appeared to be a parlor. The decor was as oppressive as Luciana had described, mismatched pieces that wouldn't have even been stylish in their day. Even the telephone on the claw-footed table was of an old style, connecting to the wall through a cable. Plenty of lighting suggested that the electrical systems were fully functional, though. He wondered about the wiring on the rest of the island.

Glass doors opened from the parlor onto a stone terrace. Gio stepped through and out into the fresh air, quickly taking note of where security cameras were placed so that he could avoid them. The sea breezes were bracing. As he made a careful assessment, he could see that one terrace led to the next and the next all in a row, each separated by a wall.

Leaning forward and around to the adjacent terrace he saw that it was empty, and was able to get a footing and swing himself over to it. Keeping from view, he peeked into the windows of the room there. Another parlor area with no one inside. He made his way to the next terrace, then peered into that sitting room.

Luciana! He'd know his love anywhere even though he saw her only in profile as she sat at a small desk typing into a laptop. Blood surged through his veins at the sight of her, and he could hardly wait to reunite with the kindheartedness and intelligence that lay beneath her staggering beauty.

The blond hairdo she was so proud of was pulled into a ponytail. She wore one of her conservative dresses, this one in brown, and looked ready to shake hands and have her photo taken at an official function. Maybe this was how princesses dressed every day, whether or not they had an engagement to attend. He'd have much to learn about palace life in the future.

Not wanting to scare her, he rapped lightly on one of the panes of the glass door. When she glanced up and recognition slowly took hold, tears leaked out of her eyes.

He'd kiss away each one.

She sprang out of her chair and rushed to open the door. Throwing her arms around his neck, she fluttered a hundred kisses all over his face and pulled him into the room, shutting the door behind her.

He swallowed his breath with a mixture of relief, yearning and joy beyond any jumble of emotions he had ever imagined possible. One disastrous scenario that had run through his mind before coming was that once he arrived, she'd not want any more contact with him. That she was ready to move forward with her fates and would not be open to his plan. Her response assured him otherwise.

"Gio," she cried, kissing him passionately on the lips and then holding him tight. "My Gio."

CHAPTER TEN

After they could momentarily tear themselves away from celebrating their reunion with hugs and kisses, Gio explained how he had wanted to meet with her father but that the king had refused. "I want to manufacture my biometric products here. I'll establish a production plant and a development center on Izerote."

Luciana could hardly believe Gio was really here, flesh and blood, in her sitting room at the palace. Florence seemed a world away. Her mind ping-ponged in a hundred directions. "I had the same idea! I was reminded of these factories we have on the island, and then one thought led to another. That maybe it would be good for both your business and for my people. I was going to contact you."

"With a different solution to create jobs on the island, surely your father won't force you to marry King Agustin."

Tears trickled down Luciana's cheeks again. Because Gio had thought of a way to save her from marrying a man she didn't love. How fundamentally considerate he was, even though she didn't doubt that this arrangement would benefit him, as well.

But after the shock of his arrival subsided, she reminded herself that Gio wasn't here to give her the rest of her life with the man she loved. He was on Izerote to do business. He'd made it clear that he wouldn't devote himself to a woman and was not interested in building a family. There was no cause to think he'd changed his mind simply because they had been physically intimate.

She thought of her last minute in Florence. How, as she was being escorted into the car that would take her away, she yelled out to Gio to tell him that she loved him. She'd never expected to see him again after that, but she'd wanted him to know. And she'd needed to hear herself say it out loud, if only once in her life. Gio had mouthed something back to her that she hadn't heard. What was it? She couldn't bring herself to just come right out and ask.

"I spotted the factories from the plane," Gio said. "Can we go see them?"

He needed all of the information he could

gather in order to prepare a presentation for her father. She had to think of a way to let him see those factories and decide if they were usable for his enterprise.

She dared not disappear again. And she couldn't very well call for a palace driver and exit her sitting room with Gio in tow. Hmm...

Recalling that fateful night when she'd climbed off her terrace to hike down to the shore where she'd stowed away on the supply boat, she remembered that her path took her straight past the factories. Gio could go that same way, and she'd go by car and meet him there.

"Good thinking, Princess." Gio planted a passionate kiss onto her lips before he hopped over the terrace wall like a swashbuckler in an old movie.

When Luciana told the driver where she wanted to go, he balked. "Your Highness, I don't believe there is anyone on the premises there anymore."

"Thank you, Nico. If you'll just proceed, I'll take it from there." It turned out Gio must have brought a little of Luci with him from Florence. Because the princess was finished with acquiescing to what everyone, including a palace driver, thought she should be doing.

Regardless of the outcome of her plan with

Gio, there was no turning back. If she refused to marry King Agustin, what could he and her father do? Throw her in jail? That didn't scare her. She was already in one.

Telling Nico to return for her in an hour, she found Gio on the property inspecting the buildings. Windows on all sides allowed them to get a good look into the inside of the factories. Gio was pleased that they were in good condition, and he could tell from the solar panels and lighting design that the structures were built with energy efficiency. He made guesstimates about the size of the work floors and how many assembly stations he could set up.

"This is really quite perfect," he said as he took her hand, his palm bathing her in instant warmth. Even if they were to be tied together only in business, Luciana thanked the universe that she'd at least have Gio in some way if they could bring this to fruition. Her world was a better place with him in it, even if he wasn't going to be at her side like she wished he would.

"Yes," she echoed. "Perfect." *Well, almost.*

They walked together to a grassy embankment behind the factories that overlooked the coast. She studied his profile while he looked out to the waves.

It was incongruous, his handsome face on

her island. The magnificent curls blowing in *her* sea breeze.

"Luci," he said, using the distinction in her name. "I didn't come to this idea only because it would be good for my corporation. Or even to help you get out of your forced engagement to King Agustin."

"You didn't?"

"No, *bellissima*." He turned to her and took hold of both of her shoulders. His strong hands traced their way inward to her throat and then rode upward to caress her jaw, until he held her face in his hands. "My actions are not merely intended to keep you from another man. I'm here because I want you. I won't say I want you to belong to me. Because you belong to yourself. You're more than capable of standing on your own two feet. And I want to walk beside you. I want to catch you if you fall. I want you to catch me, too."

He placed a light kiss on her lips. Luciana shivered with cold abandon when he let his hands drop from her face. Then her spirit soared again when he went down on one knee and looked up to her with a sparkle in his eyes that she'd swear was more beautiful than all the gemstones in the world.

"I thought I would never partner with someone. That I wouldn't make time, that I wouldn't trust. Until I met you. You fill me up rather than deplete me. I don't know if you heard me declare my love to you in Firenze as the car was taking you away from me. I love you. I have never loved before. And I never will again. My love is only for you."

She covered her mouth as the shock settled in. "But I am bound to live here in Izerote. Someday I will be queen."

"I've lived all over the world. I'll make my life here in order to be with you. I can adapt. Home is where you are. Our wills are strong. We can make this work. Your Royal Highness Princess Luciana de la Isla de Izerote, will you marry me?"

Luciana fell to her knees to meet him eye to eye. Mouth to mouth. "Yes, Gio, we *will* find a way. You are my one true love, too. Of course I'll marry you."

The clack of King Mario's boots against the wooden floor was thunderous even from behind his closed office door as Luciana and Gio approached.

"Princess." The attendant in the blazer with the palace insignia whom Gio had avoided earlier now marched toward them. "Please allow me to notify the king that you wish an audience with him."

"Thank you, Joaquin, but I refuse to make an appointment to speak to my own father," Luciana rebuffed him as she opened the office door.

Gio slipped in behind her and closed the heavy door until he heard it click shut.

"Luciana." The king looked up from his audible pacing across his office floor.

"Giovanni Grassi," Gio introduced himself and hurried to meet the king face-to-face, thrusting out his hand for a proper handshake.

King Mario merely looked at his hand and continued on his walking course.

"Bow," Luciana mouthed to Gio.

Bow? Gio couldn't believe such an antiquated custom was still used on this remote little island that, frankly, had no relevance on the world stage. He knew that bowing to royalty was protocol in formal settings, but he somehow expected a man-to-man shake would be more appropriate to this private meeting.

The king returned to his paces.

It was with a grinding of his teeth that Gio bowed his head. "It's a great honor to meet you, sir."

He wasn't sure if *sir* was an acceptable address, but Gio was doing the best he could.

King Mario sized him up, his approval or disapproval impossible to read.

Gio decided to forge ahead with a preemptive, "Your Highness, I do apologize that our acquaintance begins so unusually. After I received the intelligence that you were unwilling to meet with me, I took a bold action in conferencing with the princess."

The king finally stopped his pacing and stood facing Gio, crossing his arms over his chest. "Indeed."

"I hope that when I, when we—" Gio gestured to Luciana, who stood beside him "—fully explain our proposal, you'll agree that the plan benefits all concerned."

"So, you and my daughter have already mapped out the future of Izerote? Mr. Grassi, you've known of the existence of this island for exactly how long?"

"A week, Your Highness. Please allow me to explain."

King Mario said nothing, merely nodding his head once. Princess Luciana straightened her spine and made herself taller, which Gio took as a positive sign of her willingness to stand up to her father.

Fortunately, from the minute Gio had had this idea, he'd been compiling scores of information. As he talked of his plan to bring the manufacturing of his biometrics to Izerote, he was able to emphasize Grasstech's eco-friendly practices that Luciana had told him were very important to her father. They were the sticking point that had caused him to reject other propositions in the past for enterprise on the island.

The strategy appeared to be working because King Mario listened attentively. "And depending on your preferences, if you so choose we could operate the factories on a twenty-four-hour cycle, with three sets of staff working eight-hour shifts, allowing us to employ thousands of your citizens."

"Not to mention that Gio will be able to bring the highest level of technology into our homes and throughout all the other businesses on the island," Luciana chimed in.

"At my expense, sir. We'd seek to modernize Izerote on a full scale."

Luciana surprised Gio by taking his hand. Which felt so right, Gio's chest swelled.

King Mario took note of the hand-holding.

The act was a declaration of independence that was difficult for her father. Just the same, Gio was proud of his beloved for doing it.

"I suppose you two have got all of *that* figured out, as well," the king stated flatly as he gestured to their hands in each other's.

"We do."

"I love Gio, Father. I knew it from the moment I met him."

"Your Highness, I will admit that I'm an informal man. My employees address me by my first name. Most of the time I'm wearing a pair of jeans and sipping a cappuccino as I hover over a computer." Although he had donned his finest dark blue Savile Row suit to meet the king today.

Luciana smiled at the comment about the jeans. Gio's mind paraded back to their time in Florence when Luci had first bought the pairs of baggy jeans that she was so thrilled to wear while they took in the sights.

He and his love locked eyes, making the world disappear. With her gazing at him like that, the affection and closeness they'd come to share, Gio could conquer the world.

"I'm well aware that as a commoner, sir, I have a lot to learn about palace etiquette. Therefore, again I beg your forgiveness if I'm not following royal decorum when I ask you for your daughter's hand in marriage."

"You are already engaged." King Mario's glare could shatter glass.

"To a man that I don't love."

"Perhaps you will in time, child."

"I'm not a child and I could never love

King Agustin. Because I love Gio and there would never be any room in my heart to love another. Father, I know that you and Mother didn't have the kind of romantic love that only the lucky few are destined for. But I've been chosen. Don't you think that brings its own duty? Even though you didn't have it, don't you want that for me? I believe my mother would have."

The king's face transformed dramatically, morphing into one of a much softer man, changing into a loving father.

"I know this is a lot to take in all at once, Father. May we please sit down together?" She pointed to the dark wood conference table and chairs in front of the bay windows. "We want to tell you so much more about our plan for Grasstech on Izerote."

An hour later, Gio didn't know whether King Mario had admitted defeat or had been simply won over by his and Luciana's enthusiasm. There had been enough of the occasional half smiles and several nods indicating his comprehension of the plan that Gio was satisfied. He wanted to conclude the meeting while things were still going well.

Just one more part of the endeavor needed to be outlined. "King, there's a final matter we need to discuss."

* * *

"How do I look?" Gio buttoned his jacket and modeled for Luciana as they prepared for the public address.

She lifted up on tiptoe to give her handsome fiancé a kiss on his mouth before she applied her lipstick. "My love, you look as fine in your bespoke suits as you would in a tuxedo or in swim trunks." And added with a wink, "Or in nothing at all."

"I can't believe how nervous I am. I've spoken in public many times before."

"It's the palace balcony bit. Intimidates the best of us."

Allowing a royal dresser to approve them as they passed through the corridor, the princess and her soon-to-be husband were escorted to the inner chamber that led to the official balcony. Luciana could hear the murmur of the citizens on the grounds below. It was a din she'd heard often enough to be able to estimate that it was a packed crowd with most of Izerote in attendance.

She had to admit to some jitters herself, as she generally appeared beside her father as a porcelain doll who merely waved and rarely spoke. Today, she had a lot to tell her subjects.

King Mario joined them and they were announced as His Royal Highness King Mario de la Isla de Izerote, Her Royal Highness Princess Luciana and honored guest Mr. Giovanni Grassi of Florence.

Gio looked to Luciana for instruction, and she pointed for him to step out onto the balcony. The crowd below stretched as far as the eyes could see. With the palace grounds not able to hold the mass, people stood all the way back to the entrance lawn in order to get a glimpse of the royal family when they took to the balcony. Their appearance was met with loyal applause and cheers.

Luciana peered down to the people and worked to spot individual faces in the crowds. A young father held his toddler up on his shoulders, the boy's arms wrapped around his neck. Teenaged girls looked up to Luciana with palpable admiration. An older couple linked arms.

Truly, Luciana loved Izerote. The untamed natural beauty. The cordiality and goodness of its people. She slanted her eyes sideways to steal a glance at Gio. With this man by her side, she could do her duty to these citizens. As a pair they would not only change the island for the benefit of these deserving people, they'd leave a future of stewardship and prosperity for generations to come. Luciana again focused on the little boy atop his father's shoulders in the crowd.

"Princess." King Mario leaned in to speak only to his daughter. "You've forced me to see how much my own fear has suffocated you. I love you, daughter. You've become a wise woman. You'll make a fine queen someday."

"I love you, too. Dad." The corners of both of their mouths tipped up in a private almost smile that they alone shared.

King Mario then thrust his shoulders back and faced his subjects.

"Thank you, citizens of Izerote, for joining us today," he spoke through the standing microphone placed on the balcony. The crowd cheered. The king explained the arrangement he'd made with Grasstech to create jobs and futures for the island's population. He invited Gio to speak.

"My father began Grasstech forty years ago," he began, "at a time when computer technology was ancient compared with what it is today. He founded the company with the command to his employees to think deep, to think wide, to think far outside of the box. King Mario has told you a bit about what we plan to do here in Izerote. But, in reality, that is only the beginning. We don't yet know how high we can fly, how fast we can soar. I can hardly wait for us, together, to find out."

The throng roared with approval. Luciana filled with pride at Gio's inspiring words.

Now it was her turn to stand in front of the microphone. She peeked over to Gio, then took her place in the center of the balcony, righteous and strong.

"I am pleased to see so many children here." She pointed to six or so in her sight. "Because any actions we take today affect them tomorrow. Gio has outlined our plans to bring living wages and enduring jobs to our people. As parents, and as future parents, we understand that in order for us to be successful in our work, we need to know that our children are being meaningfully looked after. That's why I'm pleased to announce the formation of the Luci Foundation, a new initiative that will create free, quality child care for our youngest citizens until they are old enough to go to school."

Many in the audience applauded, especially the women.

Luciana bowed her head to her father, who, after she and Gio laid out their intentions for this element of the plan, had consented.

"In addition to devoting myself to you as a monarch," she continued, "it has always been my own personal dream to work with young children. To help parents raise confident, happy, creative and secure children who will grow into the big-thinking adults Gio just spoke of. I ask you today to support me in my quest. I would like to continue my education to earn an advanced degree in early childhood education so that I can lead the Luci Foundation with experience and expertise, and work together with you to bring Izerote the progress and prosperity I know we can achieve."

Her speech was met with ovations of endorsement.

In reality, Luciana had always known that her father was wrong when he insisted that the citizens of the island did not want advancement and modernization. It was only he who feared it. The protective king didn't want to put his people, or his daughter, in danger and thought that by keeping them sheltered and separate he could better safeguard them.

She and Gio would teach him. Slowly, in a way that was comfortable to him.

Her lovely Gio had already broken the ice when after the meeting in the king's office yesterday, the conversation turned friendly and Gio taught his future father-in-law how to check the weather and the world's stock markets on his smartphone.

King Mario handed something to Gio, who nodded knowingly. She'd spied them having a private tête-à-tête this morning but didn't know what the topic was.

His Royal Highness moved to the microphone. "Our family has another announcement to make. Princess Luciana has made a change in her personal plans. She will not be marrying King Agustin de la Isla de Menocita. I spoke with the king this morning and he wishes everyone on our island peace and prosperity in the future."

A hush of shock swept across the gathering. Luciana swallowed hard, knowing that she was perhaps disappointing people with this news. She was compelled to take over the microphone from her father and speak candidly.

"Are any of you in love?" she asked her subjects. Bellows and yelps came from different areas of the grounds. Couples kissed. Others smiled. "I hope you'll agree that there's no predicting love. Quite unexpectedly, I have fallen in love. To a man I wish to marry. Although he is a commoner, I hope that you will accept him and learn to love him as much as I do. Together, we will earn your trust. Ladies and gentlemen, Mr. Giovanni Grassi is not only the genius mind who will help us take our island into the next generation and beyond, he is also the man I will marry and bear children with."

Gio stepped forward and opened his hand. It held Luciana's great-grandmother's wedding ring. She remembered the family stories about Esmerelda being the only one in her lineage who fell in love with her husband after an arranged marriage.

Luciana mouthed *Thank you* to her father.

Her fiancé placed the ring on her finger.

The princess took his hand in her left and her father's in her right. The three faced the crowd, who went wild with well-wishes.

Gio and Luciana had their first official kiss as an engaged couple, which was welcomed with resounding cheers that echoed all the way to the blue skies above.

* * * * *

If you enjoyed this story,
check out these other great reads
from Andrea Bolter

Her Las Vegas Wedding
Her New York Billionaire

All available now!